young light

SEAGULL WORLD LITERATURE

RALF ROTHMANN
young light

TRANSLATED BY WIELAND HOBAN

LONDON NEW YORK CALCUTTA

 GOETHE-INSTITUT

This publication was supported by a grant from the Goethe-Institut India

Seagull Books 2010

Ralf Rothmann, *Junges Licht: Roman*
© Suhrkamp Verlag, Frankfurt am Main 2004

Published for the first time in English by Seagull Books 2010

Translation © Wieland Hoban 2009

ISBN 978 1 9064 9 754 5

British Library Cataloguing-in-Publication Data
A catalogue record for this book is available
from the British Library

Typeset and designed by Seagull Books, Calcutta, India
Printed at Leelabati Printers, Calcutta, India

Here is the night,
The night has begun;
And here is your death
In the heart of your son.

L. Cohen

Below ground everything is quiet around this time, when nobody is in the shaft or the last level yet, and the man pushed the grate shut and put the bolt down, then took a step back. Quieter than above the clouds. He opened the telephone box, took out the receiver and gave his tag number, the drift and the starting time of his shift. Once they had been confirmed he hung up, and for a few moments the steel cables moved without a sound; then the cage gave a jolt, the grates rattled and the lamp under the tin roof shook so hard that it made the dead flies in the frosted glass bowl jump. After the incline, a section of a few metres, the sounds stopped, and the elevator glided almost silently until it arrived under the arch of shale and marl; a moment later it had vanished. All that could be heard from the shaft was a high-pitched, gradually fading sound.

The drift lighting was only turned on at the start of the early shift, which would be in about 20 minutes, and the man fastened his belt, pulled his leather apron straight and checked his trouser pockets. Yardstick, pencil, logbook. Then he buttoned up his thick canvas jacket and turned on his headlamp. For a while he listened. In the distance he could hear something like wind, the fresh air in the ventilation shaft. He took the bottle from his toolbox, drank a mouthful of cold tea, then walked down the gentle slope of the level. The rock was wet; he took heavy steps with his climbing boots, and the nearby stable shafts seemed to send the reverberations of his steps and the clicking of the stones or grounding clamps he kicked up around him. At times it sounded as if he were walking towards himself.

Behind a bend where a disused scraper stood, the level dropped more steeply: a good 25 degrees. Here the tracks were cemented in, and he sat on his leather rear flap and slid some of the way down the drift, keeping his speed down with his heel caps. The water at the bottom came up to his ankles, and he had only taken a few steps when it started trickling into his shoes. He shuffled over to the first safety props of the coal face, took the little hammer out of the yardstick pouch and tapped on the steel caps—up to the chalk marking from the   previous day. They all had enough tension, and he opened his logbook, made a note and started counting the props, the work from the last shift. He saw at once that there were not enough, and, before he had noted anything down, he also realized why.

Above him, between some crevasses of a few inches' width, hung a four-metre sandstone slab and water dripped out through a fissure in thin streams. The drops sparkled like beads in the light of his lamp, and, as the man moved closer, his shoe hit something that quite obviously didn't belong there—perhaps a ball of wire. He bent down to throw it aside. It was one of the small cages that some miners kept bringing with them, in spite of the ban; it was squashed, rusted and, of course, empty. A rat trap. He threw it into the stope, and then he heard it—only quietly, but so clearly that there could be no doubt. Slowly he turned around. The bare scratches on the props flashed in the light of his lamp. Dust swirled through the beam. The sandstone ceiling above him, slanted like a roof, wasn't moving; the fissure was still the same. But suddenly the water stopped and the trickling fell silent—though only for the duration of one, maybe two, heartbeats. And then continued as before.

It was the first day of the holidays, that gentle, slightly incredulous awakening in the sun, which was shining on my bed at an angle through the pot plants. I yawned, kneeled on the pillow and drew the curtains a little further apart, slowly, to avoid making any sound. Sophie was still sleeping. She had her thumb in her mouth, and on her little finger I saw the shine of some of my mother's nail varnish.

Under the fruit trees in the garden lay some toys: a plush dog, some little moulds made from tin plates and furniture from the dolls' kitchen. The axe was leaning against the fence. Behind the rhubarb and the currant bushes, the turf-covered, clay-yellow path wound its way past the fields—oats and wheat. The awns took on a silver sparkle when the wind brushed against them, and the poppies at the field's edge also swayed a little, their petals flapping back and forth. A few birds flew as if startled across the freshly-chipped Fernewaldstrasse, disappearing behind the silos and conveyor belts that protruded from the gravel pit. On the tip of the excavator arm sat a falcon.

There was no one in the neighbouring garden either, and little Schulz's sandpit was in the same condition as the previous evening: a labyrinth of roads that led across mountains and through tunnels, inhabited by the Matchbox cars I had given him—a shoe carton of them. I had just kept the little old-timer, a Mercedes Silver Arrow. There was laundry on the clothesline in the Breuers' garden, and the water that sometimes still dripped onto the grass from the towels, bras or upturned shirts gleamed almost white, like drops of fresh light. I slipped into my khaki trousers and left the room barefoot.

The door to my parents' bedroom was open, and the beds had been made. In the bathroom, which had no windows, only a small air vent, there was no one—at least, there was no light behind the wave glass in the upper part of the door. As I pushed down the handle, however, I felt a sudden resistance, and my mother cleared her throat. She put some sort of little bottles or sticks on the shelf under the mirror and I went into the living room. The radio was on, the scale with the city names was glowing in the shady room; but the music was barely audible. Next to the sofa, the bulging arm-rest my father laid his head on when he was watching television, stood an empty beer bottle. The floorboards, painted a reddish brown, creaked quietly. Our kitchen, like my room, was on the same side as the garden, and the window was open. A cigarette was glowing in a bowl on the sideboard; the white smoke trail climbed almost vertically, then suddenly dissolved into a grey tangle. The coffee pot on the cold coal stove, with its red and violet flowers, shone in the sunlight. The lid, long broken, had been replaced with a saucer.

The glass door that led from the kitchen to the veranda—though we called it the balcony—was also open, and I leaned over the stone balustrade and looked down onto the Gornys' yard. There were large cups on the table, one of them missing its handle, and Wolfgang placed a tray full of bread, honey and margarine between them. He was my age, and so far we had been in the same class. But he was going on to high school after the holidays, and I swung myself onto the balustrade and squeezed a little saliva through the cracks between my teeth. The sound caught his attention; he cast a glance into the garden, then craned his neck and looked up at me.

'Don't you dare!' He raised a fist. 'I'll tell your mum!'

'Don't shit yourself, man. Are you coming along to the animal club later?'

He shook his head and distributed the breakfast boards, which were full of dents along the edges.

'I'm not playing any more. You tricked me. If I make a contribution, I want to join in with everything.'

'What do you mean? You can.'

'Yeah, right. And what about last week? You roasted the pigeon, and I didn't even get a bone.'

'If you're too late . . .'

'I was on time! Fattie had promised I could slaughter it. I paid for it.'

'Oh, forget it.' I dangled a leg. 'The critter tasted like a burnt tyre. We gave it to the dog.'

'It was still my loot. You're crooks.' He looked up again. The parting in his hair was dead straight, and his pale face looked as sharp as a knife. 'Hey! I hope you're coming down from there soon!'

'Who, me? Are you crazy?'

He walked around the table and laid knives between the boards, one after another, like numerals on a round watch face. 'This is our house.'

'So what? I'll piss on your head in a minute, you loser.'

'I'd like to see you try.' He vanished into the kitchen. 'You wouldn't dare!'

I leaned as far as I could to the side, aimed for his chair and released a long drop of spittle; but it smacked onto the stone floor, which was as grey as the bread. The Gornys never ate rolls.

There was a window on the other side of the veranda, just above the table and the two chairs, and I stepped down from the balustrade and pressed my nose against the glass, trying to see through the gap between the curtains. But I couldn't make anything out. The room was really part of our home; it had a separate entrance and a washbasin, and one day I was supposed to get it. But it was still rented out to a subtenant. I went into the kitchen, opened a packet of cornflakes and poured them onto the plate. A few of them fell to the ground—I quickly swept them under the stove with my foot, and took a bottle of milk from the fridge. Then I sat down at the table on the balcony, and, as I ate my breakfast, I looked out over the garden and the fields to Dorstener Strasse which had already filled with trucks. On the other side of the mounds I could see crows circling the winding tower, its wheels moving in contrary motion like the coach wheels in Bonanza.

My mother came into the kitchen, and I suppose she didn't notice me at first; the balcony was narrow, and the roof placed it in the shade. She stepped in front of the sideboard and put out the cigarette, the butt. Then she took a new one from the packet and lit up. Back then she smoked Chester, and I didn't like the yellow packaging at all. But she didn't want Gold-Dollar any more; she found it ugly when tobacco crumbs stuck to her lipstick, which was true. And they stained her fingers. She was wearing a white blouse, the skirt from her grey suit and light grey stilettos, looking dreamily out of the window while the smoke poured from her nose.

Behind the wheat field one could make out part of the unpaved road that led to Kleekamp. It was almost always empty; hardly anyone had a car, and sometimes one saw people from the home for singles practising their bike-riding there. They were Portuguese and Sicilians, former fisherman and farmers, now in the mine, and most of them had never sat on a bike before. And when they practised, constantly wobbling and falling over, it was a source of amusement to those of us on the housing estate who were watching from our balconies— even my father, who hardly ever smiled, laughed so hard one evening about a particularly clumsy one of them that Sophie had tears in her eyes.

My mother felt her hair carefully, as if she were checking her silhouette. She had got herself a new perm at the weekend, and her nails were freshly varnished.

'I'm here.' I spoke very quietly to avoid waking anyone behind the window, and she nodded, but continued staring out over the field. She was wearing her coral necklace.

'I know. Have you had breakfast?' And without waiting for my answer: 'Then take off your trousers right now so I can wash them. There's a fresh pair in the wardrobe. And this morning you're staying with your sister, you hear? I'm going into town.'

'But I wanted to go to the animal club!'

'You can still do that later. I'll be back around one.'

'So late . . . ? I'm supposed to meet them. Come on, it's the holidays.'

'Exactly. So you have enough time on your hands to do something for me for a change. I have to go for a check-up. And that's final.' Her cheekbones twitched. There were a lot of those delicate veins known as spider veins, and she turned on the tap, held the barely-smoked Chester under the water and threw it in the coal scuttle. Then she left the room.

I put a fresh plaster on my hand; it didn't hurt any more. Two days ago I hadn't done my homework, which usually led to severe punishment: one had to stretch out one's fingers, and then Dey, the teacher, lifted his arm and brought his ruler smacking down on them. It was made of wood, with a metal edge, and the number of strokes was announced in advance; there was one extra for withdrawing one's hand. The pain was so incredible that even the most hardened boys had tears in their eyes.

Dey—Crooked Dey, as we called him—had summoned me to the blackboard to take down the sums he dictated. Some of the others had raised their hands before that, but most of the time he shook his head. 'First the less able mathematicians.' And while I stared at the numbers and picked the paper off the chalk, I heard the clicking fingers of the eager ones behind me, the ones who didn't have any trouble with all this; the longer I stood there helpless, the louder they became. I drew up my shoulders, closed my eyes and nibbled at my lip, but Dey didn't put me out of my misery. He waited. I wiped the sweat from my temples with chalky fingers, and then he finally gave his usual sigh of 'Hopeless . . .' and dragged me through the room by my ear. He opened my book and showed me which exercises I had to do for the next lesson.

Then I sat at the living-room table for a long time. 'Determine the central angle . . .' I draw garlands in the margin. 'Divide the digit sum by the quotient of . . .' I carved patterns in the pencil with my thumb. The wood smelled the way I imagined Lebanon did, and I rode through the cedar forests on my white Arabian. 'If seven cubic metres of granite are extracted from a mine every day, and the relation between the specific weight of the stone and the price per ton is such that in six working days . . .' I bent over the table, laid my head on my crossed arms and fell asleep.

But my mother woke me up.

'What's all this? Are you finished?'

I nodded, closed my exercise book and took the bag to my room. Then I leafed through some old *Prince Valiant* comics that were lying on my bed and looked for the bit with Oron the Giant. I was very fond of him. He looked scary, with swellings and bumps all over. But he was good-natured, and couldn't bear the fact that humans were afraid of him. So he withdrew to places where no one wanted to live, the swamps or the reeds, and, in time, he became as shaggy and grey as the withered stalks. He had caves and shelters everywhere, knew all the usable paths in the deadly moor, lived off fish and mushrooms and didn't need anyone else. Only sometimes, about every ten or fifteen years, when his knife had become blunt, Prince Valiant came by and brought him a new one.

My mother was hanging up laundry in the garden with Sophie, and I went to the bathroom, locked the door and had a pee. Then I opened the mirror cabinet, the side with my father's things: a plastic cup, a toothbrush with a wooden handle and squashed bristles, a bottle of Irish Moss aftershave. The razor was slightly rusted, but there was a new packet of blades. I pulled one out, carefully unwrapped the waxed paper and sat down on the edge of the bathtub.

Downstairs I could hear Sophie, her gleeful laughter—almost a squeaking—then little Schulz's mouth organ, and with one edge of the blade I made a cut in the ball of my thumb, only very gently, but even that already hurt. Oron, with the tip of an enemy's arrow in his leg, had also once operated on himself and hardly batted an eyelid. I was taking fast breaths with my mouth wide open, and kept going over the skin until the edge of the razor blade disappeared into the flesh. Now the line turned red. It was a good four centimetres long, but the blood wasn't even running over the edge; I clenched my teeth and pressed harder, millimetre by millimetre. But I was already trembling all over, started farting and broke out in a sweat. Finally, my fingers grew so tense that I had to stop.

I rinsed my hand under the tap and looked at the ball of my thumb. A nasty scratch, but not a wound. I went to the kitchen, took a match from the box and rubbed the sulphur head about inside the cut until my eyes watered. Then I put a plaster on it, wiped the bathroom floor with toilet paper and told my mother I had fallen over. At night, before going to sleep, I could feel a quiet throbbing under the bandage.

But I didn't have a fever the next morning . . . In school, Crooked Dey drew the curtains, the sun bathed the room in orange light, and he went from table to table, checking our homework and making a note here and there. I was the only one who didn't have his exercise book open, and Godtschewski, my neighbour, gave me a nudge. But I kept it shut.

Dey was just giving Tszimanek the treatment; he took the ruler out of his pocket and pressed it up against the boy's chest.

'Mathematics is not so bad. It can even be fun. Because it's not just there to calculate gains and losses, but also to sharpen our logical faculty.' He twirled the hair at his temples. 'Do you believe that?'

Tszimanek bared his teeth, and my neighbour gave me another nudge, pointing to the exercise book.

'What's up?' he whispered, and I turned my hand so that he could see the plaster.

'Couldn't write.' I picked at one corner until it came unstuck. 'Injured myself.'

Carefully I removed it. The ball was swollen and red, and the wound had a crust of clotted blood that made it look wider than it was. There was a little pus oozing from its edges, and I kept my fingers slightly bent, as if the tendons were already inflamed.

Godtschewski gaped at it and puffed up his cheeks, then shook his head. 'But you're right-handed.'

He grinned, and I too twisted my mouth; but I stopped breathing for a moment. I felt a sudden wave of heat going through my face, then I felt queasy and I was no longer aware of the hissing and whispering all around me and the turning of pages in books. I stared at my hands as if they belonged to someone else. Holding the razor blade with my left hand to cut my writing hand—I hadn't thought of that at all, not even for a second. I stuck the plaster under the bench and looked around. Dey was standing two rows behind me.

I raised my arm and clicked my fingers. He looked up. There was chalk on his tie; he had grey hairs in his nose.

'Well?'

'Can I please leave the room?' My voice sounded shaky. 'I'm feeling sick.' He reached into the breast pocket of his jacket and took out a pair of rimless glasses. Now his eyes seemed to sparkle, and once he had taken a look at me he glanced quickly at my exercise book. 'Then go to the loo. But you'll be back here in two minutes.'

The hallway was deserted, and the sound of my soles smacking against the floor echoed in the stairwell as if it were high above me. The smooth wood of the banister was nice and cool. I didn't want to cross the schoolyard where the whole class could see me, and ran under the canopy of the sports hall, past a long wall of glass bricks, to the gate. Voices behind it, the calling and shrieking of girls playing dodgeball, and sometimes I caught sight of a black sports shirt or an arm, maybe a leg, distorted as if behind clear ice.

I ran to the copse at the edge of the housing estate, planted not long ago on rubble and gravel pits; there was no one here either at this time of day. There was a gurgling stream in the dip between the elder bushes, a rust-coloured rivulet that rushed through a concrete bed, and I jumped back and forth between the left bank and the right, keeping an eye out for frogs. Insects were dancing in the sunbeams that came in at an angle through the foliage, and further up someone had built a waterwheel out of a thick cork and pieces of a cigar crate. It was turning so fast in the current that a small cloud of white spray was forming, with the trace of a rainbow arching above it.

When I came to the Kleekamp gang's tree house I stopped for a moment. Not a sound, no voices; just to be on the safe side, I threw a stone onto the cardboard roof, but there was no reaction. The house was built on two not very tall oak trees that had grown together into a crooked tangle, and if one pulled oneself up by the lower branch, the others could be used as a staircase. In front of the entrance was a small platform with a box of withered sweet peas on it, and on the curtain, a woollen blanket full of holes, there was a cardboard sign that read: 'Whoever gos in here is ded.'

They even had a cooking stove in the house, a hollowed-out cavity block, and on the surrounding benches lay plastic plates, rinsed mustard glasses and a hubcap, which was the ashtray. In the corner there was a bucket hanging on the wall, containing a handleless frying pan, a poker and a few spoons, and there were candles—mostly reduced to stumps—stuck on the sawn-off branches; the ceiling above them was black with soot. I rummaged in the box under the window, but found only a few empty beer bottles and an issue of the *Sankt-Pauli-Nachrichten* that I already knew. But I flicked through it anyway. Almost all the women had breasts like Frau Latif, our art teacher; sometimes hers touched us when she bent down to correct something. The paper stained my fingertips.

I wiped them on my trousers, and then I suddenly heard something below me, a cracking and rustling. One could look through the floor, through the cracks and holes. But I didn't see anyone, so I crawled to the entrance and pushed the curtain aside a little, just the lower edge. Bushes and trees, a butterfly among the ferns. Silver spiders' threads. But there had to be someone down there; small branches cracked underfoot like little knucklebones, and these shoes certainly weren't a child's. Least of all one playing cowboys and Indians. A bird flew out of the grass into the alder trees with an angry twittering.

RALF ROTHMANN

Then it was suddenly quiet, and I—still on all fours—didn't make a single move. My pulse was pounding in my ears. Finally I heard a splashing and pattering, sounding slightly different every time, like water falling on old leaves, soft moss or hard, sandy soil, and just then the smell of fresh piss wafted up to me. A moment later I saw a light blonde shock of hair and heard the sound of a zip with its fine little teeth.

The man scratched the bald patch on the back of his head and looked across the area in front of the trees, across piles of building rubble between which stood the burnt-out wreck of an Isetta. The leather bag he was carrying was old and covered in scratches, and as he bent down I saw the dandruff on the shoulders of his jacket. He lifted up a piece of a blue tile and threw it onto an old stage lamp lying in the middle of the clearing. It was so rusty that the shard cut right through the tin exterior.

He probably didn't stay under the tree for very long, but it felt like an eternity to me. It was tiring to breathe silently, and my nose was still blocked from crying. My hand, the wound, was throbbing and, although my knees hurt on the hard floorboards, I remained motionless so as not to give myself away. But there was a cracking sound nonetheless; a gust of wind had moved the cardboard roof, and the man seemed to stop short and looked around. And then, as if it had only just occurred to him that there might also be someone above him, he lifted his head slowly, almost carefully. His forehead was full of wrinkles, his eyebrows were arched, and from where I was it looked as if the tips of his shoes were growing out of his chin. There was a dirt ring around the collar of his nylon shirt.

I knew he couldn't see me in my dark cave; I had often thought myself that the tree house was empty, and then the curtain had barely been lifted before one was greeted by a hail of missiles fired from tubes, slingshots or pea-shooters. And it was probably because I was seeing the man's face—his thin mouth, narrow nose and bright eyes—upside down that I only realized when I heard his voice, with the muted, but gruff order 'Come down from there!', that it was Herr Gorny, our landlord.

I said nothing, and hardly breathed. He couldn't see me. And it was unlikely that he would climb up by the oak's lower branches; they were too thin to support an adult. So I kept still and didn't move my head even a millimetre, to make sure I didn't lose the view I had of him through the crack in the floorboards. Because I was so terrified of being asked why I wasn't in school, it didn't occur to me to wonder why he was out in the heath at this time of day rather than below ground. He snuffled, took a step to the side, and I also moved my head and peeped through the next gap.

His nose was bent slightly to the left, and his eyes were close together—something my mother couldn't stand. Eyes like that are a sign of stupidity, she said whenever there was trouble with him; like the other day, when he had forbidden my father to set up a dovecote on the roof. And his mouth always looked as if he were trying to pull the skin on the inside of his lips through the cracks between his teeth, even now, while he seemed to be checking every knothole and every furrow in the ground. He kept one hand in his trouser pocket while doing so, and rummaged about in it as if he were looking for something. I heard some coins or keys.

Finally he spat on the ground, one tiny drop, and left through the clearing. He didn't seem to be in any hurry, and when his head had disappeared behind the hills, the weed-ridden rubble heaps, I quietly counted to 20. It was only after I finished counting that I climbed down from the tree. The urine stain on the bark looked like the shadow of a tombstone, and I undid my shorts and pissed past its edges.

Behind the heath there was a children's play-ground, and I sat down on one of the swings. But my legs had grown too long to get very high; if I stretched them out, they hit the ground on the way down. I went to the kiosk and gathered up the cigarette butts in front of the steps. I did the same at the bus stop, then turned off onto the narrow path between the estate and the fields. The grass brushed against my calves; the leaves of the red poppies were cool. I sat down on the rusted sheaf-binder that stood there and crumbled the tobacco onto a piece of newspaper, which yielded a fat, far too loosely rolled cigarette; I drew the flame into my mouth.

The clock struck 12 as I made my way home, keep-ing to the path along the gardens. From the open kitchen windows I heard the rattling of dishes and cut-lery; at the Kaldes' it smelled of Maggi sauce, at the Urbans' of onions, and I managed to reach our front door without meeting anyone from my class. For some reason the steps seemed higher than usual. The door of the apartment was open. My mother was standing in front of the sideboard, layering cooked pasta in a casserole, and didn't respond to my quiet, almost whispered 'Hello'. At least, not with a greeting.

'Wash your hands!'

She hardly looked up from her work, and I nodded, but didn't move. My spittle tasted strange, almost rotten, and I scratched at the scab of the wound, which was suddenly itching. The glasses in the cupboard shook slightly as a car, probably a truck, drove past the house. My bag was on the sofa, and the maths exercise book lay in the fruit bowl. My mother looked around. There was a dark strand dangling in front of her eyes, and she brushed it aside with the back of her hand. 'Now!'

In the bathroom I pushed the door shut and was going to turn the key, but she had removed it. I drank a mouthful of water from the tap and sat down on the toilet, as I suddenly had diarrhoea, just a little. And not as loud as I would have liked. Then I pulled the chain and soaped my hands, which took a while, as the soap, which was old and already partly cracked, didn't work up a proper lather anymore. I rinsed them, washed them again, and as I reached for the towel I looked at my face in the mirror. It was pale, almost as pale as my little sister's was last year after the operation. I opened the cabinet and took out the file, then cleaned my nails. But I hadn't even finished the first thumb when my mother pushed down the door handle—as abruptly as if she had struck it with her fist.

She tilted her head a little, and her eyebrows, those painted arches, almost came together above the bridge of her nose. I walked past her into the hall, and just heard her replacing the key, which she had probably hidden in her apron, in the lock. In the living room I turned up the radio, and for a moment I had the feeling that my mother's steps were becoming distant. But then she was suddenly behind me, and pushed me through the doorway and into the kitchen, where it smelled of sweet tomato sauce and freshly chopped parsley.

'Why did you run out of school?' She rummaged in the drawer and pulled out a wooden spoon. Everything around my mouth was so soft that I could hardly even form a word. But she understood anyway. 'So what? Why *shouldn't* he hit you? It serves you right if you don't do your homework. It was just the same for us.' She turned round and put out the cigarette that was smoking away in the ashtray. Her eyes took on a frozen, vacant look, as if she didn't see me at all, and the next moment she grabbed the back of my neck, laying her hand around it like a vice.

Even though I had just peed, the first smack made me lose a little urine and fall to the ground. She normally beat me until she didn't have the strength to carry on, and I couldn't shake her resolve this time either with my cries, which became more like shrieks with every blow.

'Please don't! Don't, Mum!' She got faster and faster, like when she beat carpets, and sometimes she also hit my naked thigh; and when the wooden spoon broke into pieces, she carried on with her hand. It was only when she heard the doorbell, just a very short ring, and Frau Gorny called her and asked for a cup of flour through the crack of the open door, that she stopped, pushed the splinters under the stove with the tip of her shoe, and turned round.

'But of course, my dear Trude, just a moment. Do come in!' She cooled off her arm under the tap, then I stood up and went to the living room and turned the radio off.

Some wasps had landed on the plate and were drinking from a drop of milk, and I pushed my feet against the balustrade on the balcony and looked up to the sky. An aeroplane was pulling a banner through the cloudless blue. 'Men like us cheer: Wicküler beer!' I heard the Gorny children quarrelling on the terrace. Over pork sausage or honey, as always. The Gornys never ate anything else. With that some rye bread and decaf, every morning and every evening, and Frau Gorny, who came from Austria and was very fat, took the sausage away from her children, the whole ring, tore it into several pieces and laid it on their breakfast boards. Then everything was quiet.

Although the house belonged to them, the Gornys lived in more cramped conditions than we did. The children's room, which was the same size as the one Sophie and I had, was shared by all four children—two girls and two boys—,and they didn't have a living room like ours, no armchairs or sofas or wall units, only two tables and a few corner seats of the kind one normally has in kitchens. One could lift up the top, and there were woollen blankets and games stored underneath—Ludo, Mikado and Monopoly. Behind the television in the corner stood Herr Gorny's accordion, which he played on Sunday afternoons or on birthdays. Then all the children had to join in and sing, and at the end there were thick pieces of cake, butter cream cake; Frau Gorny sometimes mixed in some black pudding because of its chocolate colour.

Herr Gorny also worked at the mine, but he was hardly ever tired when he came home from his shift. At least, not as tired as my father, who always took a nap right after supper. Uncle Harald, my mother's brother-in-law, only shook his head if someone mentioned him. 'The lazy bastard! Loafs around behind the wagons and lets the others do the work. We've already got a joke below ground: what does Gorny do just before the shift's over? He takes his hands out of his pockets.'

But he was our landlord, and while my father slept he mowed the lawn, wove roses into the fence and cultivated his fruit trees. Or he watched his children as they weeded, polished shoes or stacked firewood. The logs had to be lined up exactly, the tips of the boots weren't allowed to poke out over the edge of the shelf, and woe to any child who brought home bad grades from school. Then they had to lie down across the sawhorse, trousers around their knees, and he took his broad belt out of its loops. He struck very calmly and precisely, and one heard the smacks from the garden. But rarely more than four or five.

Behind me the curtain was drawn to the side; the rings rattled through the track. But I didn't look round, not even when someone knocked on the glass. The window frames were freshly painted, and had been baked slightly by the sun. They gave a loud crack when Marusha pulled on the handles.

'Out of the way, you rat!'

I moved my chair along and she sat down on the inside window ledge, pulled up her legs and turned round on her bottom. She was wearing red jogging trousers and a men's sleeveless vest, and put her feet on our table.

'Well? Don't I get a "good morning"?'

I nodded. Her shirt stretched across her breasts; the fabric seemed to be thinner there, and although she was only 15, she had lots of little dark hairs on her forearms. She folded them in front of her knees and yawned. She threw her head back all the way as she did, and I could see the fillings in her teeth, two of them. No, three.

'God, I slept like shit! The heat in that room! Like in an incubator. Got a cigarette?'

'Why don't you leave your window open?' Her brown curls were tousled.

'So you can get in, eh?'

'Me? Why? What would I do that for?' She wiped a little sleep from her eyes with her thumb and forefinger. Somehow she smelled of vanilla.

'Don't worry, I'd show you . . . So what about that ciggy?'

I shook my head. I liked the freckles on her nose and the little dimple in her chin, and the bluish shadows under her eyes were also nice. She was different than the other Gorny children, who all had smooth blonde hair like their father. But then, he wasn't her real father. He called her Maria. She pointed into our kitchen, to the sideboard next to the sink.

'And what's that?'

'Those are my mother's. Go ahead and ask her if she'll give you one.' She closed her eyes for a moment and smacked her lips quietly, pulling a face.

'You wouldn't believe the horrible taste I've got in my mouth . . . stay away from alcohol, I tell you!'

'What alcohol? It's much too bitter for me.'

'So you've tried it then?'

'No. Just a sip of beer from my father.'

'And sang dirty songs after that, I'll bet. Do you lot ever go on holiday?' I told her we didn't. There was a little dirt between her toes. 'And why not?'

'Why should we? You don't either.'

'Because we've got a mortgage to pay, sunshine. But you've got money, haven't you? Your mother smokes two packets a day.'

I tapped my forehead. 'She does not!' But most of the time she smoked even more than that. 'She might have to go to hospital. And that's why we can't go anywhere.'

Marusha whistled through her teeth. 'Where? Uh-oh. Are you getting a little brother?'

'Rubbish! She's having trouble with her gall bladder.'

'Ah, so that's what they call it these days.' She stretched out her arm. 'Give me your hand. No, the other one.'

'What for?'

35

She closed her fingers tightly around my wrist. 'Because I'm going to tell your future now.' She looked straight into my face, and I gulped and drew back. But Marusha was stronger, and grabbed me again with lightning speed; her silver rings hurt. The chair was only standing on two legs now. 'Listen, sweetie.' She spoke through her teeth in a muted voice. 'Because you're going to get me a fag right now, and matches to go with it. Or I'll tell your old lady . . .' She lifted an eyebrow. 'You know what!'

There was also extremely fine hair growing around the corners of her mouth. Even in the hollow between her breasts. I pulled a face, nodded, and she gave me another threatening look in the eyes and licked her lower lip. She didn't just let me go; she kept her fingernails firmly on my skin, so that I scratched myself when I pulled my arm away.

I took a step through the doorway, and was thinking of simply disappearing inside. Sophie was babbling in the bathroom. But then I knocked a Chester out of the packet after all, and rummaged about in the drawer to find some matches. There were a few books of matches from Kleine-Gunck or Grobe inside, dance halls on the outskirts of Bottrop, but I took a green one from Wienerwald and was just about to go back when my mother came into the kitchen.

'What's all this!' She hung her handbag on the door handle and pointed at my trousers. 'Didn't I just tell you to take them off? I want to start the washing machine.'

I reached back and put everything back on the sideboard. 'But which ones am I going to put on? They're the only ones I have!'

My mother frowned and cast a quick glance at the balcony. 'Rubbish! What are you talking about! The whole cupboard is full of trousers.'

'But only shorts!'

Marusha took her feet off the table and put them on the windowsill. 'Hello, Frau Collien!' Her voice was much brighter now, somehow childlike, and she smoothed her hair.

'Good morning.' My mother pulled up the corners of her lips, hinting at a smile. And then to me again: 'Of course shorts, what else. It's summer!'

'But my mates wear long trousers! Almost all of them!'

'Ah, so that's the way the wind's blowing!' She shook her head in amusement. 'My son wants to grow up . . .' She pointed at the marks on my knees. 'But then you have to act that way too, sunshine. Because big men don't slide about in the grass. At least, not in trousers.' She winked at Marusha, and the girl gave a silvery-bright giggle. 'So let 'em down!'

'Yes. In a minute.'

'No, right now! I have to go.' She pointed at the open flap of the Constructa machine and I nodded, trying to get past her into the living room. But she grabbed me by the shirt. Her head turned red, she narrowed her eyes and pushed her lower teeth forwards. But spoke very quietly. 'Hey! Are you deaf? I said take off your damned trousers!'

'Yes!' I lifted my arm in defence. 'I'm going.'

'Why? Where are you off to? The machine's *here*! You lot drive me crazy.' She reached for my belt, and I drew back. But with a jolt she pulled me into the sunlight, a slanted patch of it, then opened the buckle and the zip and pulled the trousers down over my knees. Sand poured out of the pockets.

Then she squatted down, and I held on to her shoulder and took first my left, then my right leg out of the trousers, casting a single brief glance at my neighbour.

My old, grey fine rib underpants were worn-out and patched-up; the seat of the trousers hung down low between my skinny legs, and my mother shut the flap of the washing machine and set the programme. The water tube twitched.

Marusha, who had been watching me quietly and seriously, cleared her throat and gave a sudden smile. 'Are you going out, Frau Collien?'

My mother shook her head and straightened the cuffs of her blouse. 'I wish!' She took the half-full packet of cigarettes from the sideboard and tossed it to the girl. Marusha raised her eyebrows and opened her mouth as if stunned, but caught the packet with one hand. 'Don't tell anyone, you hear?' Then she clicked her fingers and pointed to the book of matches from Wienerwald. 'Well come on then, be a gentleman. Give the lady a light!'

My sister was kneeling on the sofa and cutting figures out of an old catalogue from Klingel, in Pforzheim. She did it pretty roughly, and I took care of the detail work— the bits under the arms or between the legs of the models—with nail scissors. The table was covered with white or sky-blue snippets; some of them had prices or 'Genuine Trevira!' written on them, and Sophie looked up. She wasn't wearing her glasses. She almost never wore them.

'I'm hungry. You too?'

'Yes. Shall I get us some bread?'

'No. I want mashed potatoes with tomato sauce.'

'Then you'll have to wait until Mum comes.'

'Why? You're grown-up, aren't you, can't you cook me something too?'

'No, I can't. You know I'm not allowed to use the stove. So what do you want: sausage or cheese?'

'Raspberry jam, but later. I still have to cut out the workmen. Look at the fat one here—he looks like Grandpa Jupp.' With her tongue behind her upper lip, she curved her way around the figure with the scissors and sighed quietly when it fell out of the paper. 'Done.' Then she wiped her forehead with the back of her hand. 'Hey Julian, why don't we go on holiday anymore?'

I shrugged my shoulders. 'Because we don't have any money.'

'What do you mean? Dad earns some every week!'

'But we spend that money too; we have to eat. And then we have debts. The furniture, the TV, and all the shoes and clothes out of this catalogue here. We're growing too fast, Mum says.'

'What are debts?'

'Well, anything you have to pay. You still have some debts with me, for example—those five pfennigs for the sherbet.'

'That was old! It wasn't fizzy at all anymore . . . But I don't get it—everyone in my class goes on holiday; don't they have any debts?'

'How should I know? Look, I'll show you a trick.' I tore a figure out of the catalogue and cut off its head. It went spinning off the table, and Sophie giggled.

'What are you doing?'

It was a man dressed in an autumnal suit, and I quickly cut it out more exactly. 'Look: if you leave two flaps at the shoulders, you can fold them back and hang the suit in front of another figure. That way you can keep giving them new clothes.'

But that's a woman! She can't wear a tie.'

'Why not? And you can give the builder over there a nightie.'

'A see-through one? You can see the bra.'

'Doesn't matter.'

She grinned broadly. She had a double chin for a moment, and wasn't as pale as usual. I looked at the clock on the cupboard.

'Damn, it's already two. She was supposed to be here ages ago.'

'Perhaps she's buying us something. Just go!'

'That's easy for you to say. You don't know what those wooden spoons taste like. Don't you want to come along? I'll make us a sandwich to eat on the way, and we could . . .'

She shook her head. 'It stinks in your clubhouse; I don't want to go there. The fat one's stupid, he always pushes me around.'

'Not if I'm there. I have to feed the animals, you know. It's my turn. They're as hungry as you are.'

She pushed a few pieces of cut-out furniture around on the glass panel: kidney-shaped tables, cock-tail armchairs, phonographs. 'I'm hungrier. Can you make me some fettuccine? One can have them with sugar too.'

'I already told you: I'm not allowed to light the stove! But there's a fireplace in front of the animal club. We'll take a few potatoes and roast them, just like last year on the camping trip, you remember?'

'Really?' She looked up. The reddish curls were fixed above her forehead with a clasp—three plastic currants—,and once again she shook her head and pulled a face. 'Why can't we go on a trip, Julian? Everyone in my class goes on holiday.' I could sense that she was about to cry.

'I'm not so sure they do. They're only saying that to show off. None of my mates go on holiday either. They're all here, in the animal club.'

'Rubbish! Just Fattie and the stupid Marondes. They put a carrot in my knickers.'

'What?! That was just a bit of fun.'

'No it wasn't. It was disgusting. There was earth and some little animal sticking to it!'

The first tears fell onto the cut-out figures. 'I want to go on holiday now! I've got some sunglasses, a swimsuit, and Dad gave me the red suitcase. Why can't we go?'

'Come on . . .' I looked at the clock again. 'You're hungry. You should stop crying. Where do you want to go anyway?'

But all she could do now was cry. She let herself fall back into the cushions and laid one arm across her eyes. 'How should I know! Somewhere with horses. And a lake to go swimming.'

'We could go to the quarry pond.'

'No! There are shards in there!'

'You're right, I forgot about that. But please stop crying now! There's no reason at all. Wipe your tears away. Wipe them away. Maybe Mum'll send us to a holiday park on the outskirts.'

Sophie sniffled. 'What for?' She pulled one of her teddies out from under the pillow, the little shaggy one. His name was Muck. 'We live on the outskirts!'

'Sure, I know. But there's another side, and they've got swimming pools, pony rides, sack races and stuff like that over there. Maybe we can go there. Shall I sing you Maigret?' She liked it when I sang the theme tune from the series in my own way, in a sort of made-up French.

I was good at talking through my nose. But this time she didn't react, not even a shake of the head. She seemed to be listening carefully. A tear dripped from her chin.

I also heard the front door, the sound of the keys, and then my mother's steps on the stairs, much more slowly than usual. I quickly swept the snippets off the table and picked the others off the couch. But some of them fell out through my fingers.

Sophie wiped her eyes with one of her teddy's paws, and our mother opened the door and looked around the room; she was tired. She slipped out of her pumps, just left them standing there. There was a little plaster on the back of her hand. 'Well, you two? Have you eaten anything?'

Without waiting for a reply, she went into the kitchen. She lit a match, and a moment later a cloud of smoke rose and my sister stood up. 'I would like some potato pancakes with jam. And a strawberry milkshake, but well-mixed. Listen, Julian said we could go to a holiday park. Is that true?'

My mother walked through the room with her suit jacket over her arm. Her nylon stockings left damp footprints on the linoleum floor, and she reached back, opened the zip and wriggled out of the grey skirt with one or two movements of her hips. 'Why was Sophie crying?'

She looked at me. With my fingers full of snippets, I lifted my shoulders and gulped, and she stepped onto the carpet and held out her hand. I gave her the paper. One of her suspender buttons had come undone. 'Hey, what's wrong with your ears? I want to know why Sophie was crying!' In the light her eyes were blue, dark blue; but in the shady living room they seemed as black as the teddy's.

My sister picked her nose. 'Nothing, Mum, it was nothing. He wasn't annoying me, honest. I just wanted to eat something. When's Dad coming?'

The co-op was at the other end of the estate; I had to go to the end of Flöz-Freya-Strasse, then down Flöz-Röttgers-Strasse and Herzogstrasse, and the fact that all the houses looked alike was already enough to make the way seem endless. They all had narrow front yards, two brick steps that led to the green painted doors, a whitewashed ground floor and a grey first floor, and each was slightly behind the next. So Flöz-Freya-Strasse was only seemingly straight; if one turned round, all the staggered gables made it look like an accordion stretched far apart.

The co-op, Spar, was located in the only building with a flat roof. The black plaster was so rough that one could use it to grate pieces of polystyrene to a fine snow. I took the empty bottles to the drinks section and bought onions for 25 pfennigs. 'Help wanted!' read a sign next to the scales. 'Written applications only!'

Small cubes of Gouda cheese were on offer for tasting at the cheese counter; I ate a few and put the little flags in my pocket. But as I went to the checkout, I read on the bag that the onions cost 32 pfennigs, and went back again. The shop assistant, who was polishing apples with a duster, looked up at the ceiling, where round convex mirrors had recently been attached. Her silver bracelets rattled.

'Excuse me, I'm supposed to get onions for 25 pfennigs.'

She frowned. 'Well? Did I give you lemons?'

I grinned and showed her the price on the bag.

'So? Do you want me to cut them up?'

'No.' I held out the return ticket for the bottles. 'But I only have 25 pfennigs.'

She pulled one of the corners of her mouth far down into her cheek. Then she took out a particularly fat specimen, weighed everything again and wrote a new price on the bag. Eighteen pfennigs. 'Right, and now leave me alone. Got other things to do, you know.'

Under the silver I saw a reddish rash. She looked at the ceiling again, and I thanked her and went around the deep freeze and down the aisle with tinned food, pasta and pastries. The two Maronde boys were standing in front of the sweet shelf. The older one, Karl, his face full of spots, grinned at me and nodded towards his brother. Franz had torn open a box of chocolates, the kind with liqueur in them, and was stuffing them in his mouth one after the other. One could recognize the shape of the pieces through his cheek, and each time he swallowed it sounded as if he was going to vomit. But still he kept stuffing, the box was almost empty, and his brother also reached for the shelf and held out a handful of chocolate bars to me—Milky Way.

I shook my head. I pointed to the vegetable stand behind me with my thumbs, and wanted to walk past the two boys; but the aisle was narrow, and Karl simply stuck the chocolate in my shirt and turned away. I tore open my eyes and cursed him silently; every muscle in my face was tense. But he just shrugged his shoulders and made a movement with his head that I knew from the fair: piss off.

Then he stuffed a chocolate bar in his waistband, and at that very moment the hand of his brother, who was rummaging further back in the shelf, was grabbed by the shop assistant on the other side. The bracelets jingled and he pulled back, but couldn't free himself. Bags and boxes fell to the ground.

'This time I saw it! Just you wait . . . Hanni? Hannchen! I've got them! Come here!'

Franz grew pale. Brown spittle dribbled from the corners of his mouth, and he looked around for us imploringly. The clack-clack of the cashier's wooden heels hammered into my temples as she came down the aisle. Her ponytail was swinging back and forth.

'Aha!' Her lips were thin, even thinner than my mother's, and she grabbed Franz and Karl by their collars. 'I've been watching you two for a long time. This'll cost you, boys. Your parents'll be pleased, won't they!' The varnish on her fingernails had flaked off and, while she dragged the brothers to the checkout, she looked back over her shoulder. Her eyelids were blue. 'Come on!'

I didn't know whom or what she meant. The apprentice appeared at the end of the aisle, a tall guy with a bowl cut. He crossed his arms, and I bent down to pick up the chocolates that had fallen down, then replaced them on the shelf, arranged a few boxes and adjusted a price tag that was askew—when I felt the hand of the other shop assistant on my back.

'Come along now, sweetie!' She gave me a push. 'You run with the pack, you hang with the pack.'

At the checkout the Marondes had to lay the contents of their pockets on the counter: two bags of liquorice pastilles, four packets of chewing gum, three bars of chocolate, a hip flask, blended rum, and a large number of cheese cubes with their little flags. The cashier sat down on her swivel chair, made a list of everything, then put it in a basket. And finally turned to me.

I handed her the bottle return ticket and she put it on the nail next to the bell. Then she typed in the sum for the onions and gave me the change. Without touching my hand. I put it away, reached into my chest pocket and placed the chocolate bars on the table.

'And I'd like to return these.'

She grunted mockingly and leaned to the side; something was wrong with one of her sandals. She had taken it off and was fiddling with the strap.

'Well, see here, you want to return them. Good boy! But it's not quite that easy to get out of a theft. The police will have a thing or two to say about the matter.'

'But I didn't do anything!' The Maronde brothers were standing by the shelf where lottery forms were filled out, hanging their heads. The fruit saleswoman slid a book over to them; Franz wrote something in it, and I pointed to Karl, who was licking some chocolate traces from the corner of his mouth. 'He stuck them in my pocket! I met him here by chance, and he caught hold of me and . . .'

'That's enough out of you!' The cashier frowned, and her gaze was suddenly like metal. 'As if shoplifting isn't bad enough—now you're telling on your friends too? You're the worst of the lot. You should all be put in a detention centre!'

My fingers had grown damp from the heat and made the green bag soggy. I held it together in front of my chest with both hands.

'What do you mean . . . ?' The sweat was stinging in my eyes. 'I'm not telling on anyone. But my mother's sick, she has gallstones and her circulation and everything, and if the police . . . Then she'll, I mean, she has to have an operation, and if I make her worry, she might . . . I didn't do anything.'

She chuckled bitterly. 'Oh really? You should have thought about that sooner, my boy. I'd get gallstones too if I had kids like that.'

The apprentice grinned. As I wiped my eyes with my forearm, the bag tore completely, and onions fell to the ground, and I bent down and stuffed them in my trouser pockets. A fourth one rolled so far under the counter that I could hardly reach it. In fact, it was already lying under the wheels of the cashier's swivel chair, and I lay down on my front and stretched out one arm through the dust and fluff—when she moved. I would have had to reach across her foot with its varnished toenails, so I drew back my hand and left the onion there.

The women mumbled something I couldn't make out, and suddenly I heard a sound, a beeping that seemed far away, yet also inside me. The door opened, and the grey images, with a few light hairs gleaming among them, spun round once. I closed my eyes, but that only made me dizzier. The apprentice laughed, and when I got up again there were dark spots dancing in front of my eyes. Karl and Franz were gone. The cashier took a ball-point pen out of her pocket.

'All right then: as it's the first time, we'll let you off without a charge. But there'll be a letter from the management.' She handed me the notebook, which already held the names of the others, and pointed to a free space. 'Write down your address, and make sure one can read it!'

I thanked her, sniffled, and wiped my hand on my trousers. Sweat dripped onto the chequered paper, and it was only after I was finished that I saw the Marondes had pretended they were called Krüger. And the street they had named was also wrong. I clipped the pen to the book, thanked her again, and the cashier gave me a searching look. She didn't look quite so unfriendly anymore.

'Improve yourself, you hear?' Then she placed the missing onion in front of me.

'Yes,' I said, and walked out.

The man bent down, pushed the truss deeper into the bore hole and placed a hydraulic prop underneath. He did the same on the other side, braced the supports and crept backwards out of the hole. In the cross cut he had to drill to the ventilation shaft, he had unexpectedly struck coal: anthracite. He pulled the drill with its arm-length tip out of the crevasse and laid it aside. It was hot down here, over 30 degrees, but as the coal face was little more than four feet wide he had to keep his thick jacket on, or else scratch up his whole back and shoulders. Walking stooped was more strenuous than sliding along on his knees, and he strapped his kneepads on tightly, wrapped the tube twice around his upper body, and, pushing the heavy pneumatic hammer along in front of him, crawled towards the coal, towards its black gleam, which sometimes turned silver in the light of his headlamp.

In doing so, he scraped the back of his hand against the rock wall, the sharp ridges, and he reached up, adjusted the angle of his lamp, and watched for a moment as his blood mingled with the dust. Then he wiped his fist on the jacket and took his leather gloves out of the bag. The closer he came to the coal, the lower the hanging wall became; the edges and spikes scraped across the helmet, and dust and small stones poured down the back of his neck.

Once he reached it, he took off the tube, opened the air pressure valve and lifted the hammer. The chisel clicked—he pressed it against a protrusion in the rock, placed his fingers in the groove in the handle and pushed the button. There was a deafening noise, and at first his teeth clashed together. The chunks fell off to one side and broke apart, chalk marl slid down after them, and the harder the man pressed the hammer into the coal, the thicker the dust cloud became. The area was poorly ventilated.

He had not even cleared out one cubic metre before he had to stop; the beam of his lamp could hardly penetrate the dust anymore. He put down his tool, crawled back, took the hose pipe from the pump next to the hydraulic station and hosed down the coal face until the dust had settled. Then he crawled back to the drift, the vertical layers; thin mud flowed towards him, and what he saw gleaming there between the props and cap beams looked so pure in its blackness; it was a purity he had only ever seen in white objects in the daylight, for example a fresh bandage or an altar cloth. The man took off his left glove and touched the smooth surface with his fingertips.

He took the mallet from his belt, turned it around and knocked its handle against the coal, progressing slowly, hand-breadth by hand-breadth. At first everything sounded normal and solid, but then he discovered a point just above the level; something was hollow there, and he opened the safeguard and took the chisel out of the pneumatic hammer, pressed it against the coal and knocked against it carefully with the mallet until the sound changed once again. He had broken through a layer and could now turn the iron with his hand like a drill. The interstice was not deep, three or four centimetres, and as soon as the tip struck the next layer the man levered up the chisel, which initially failed. At the second attempt, however, he managed to break out the coal, which fell before his knees, and he stooped down until his headlamp illuminated the cavity.

A skeleton had been embedded in the yet untouched, gleaming black coal bed, presumably a bird; it was no larger than a child's hand, and one of its wings was twisted. Instead of a beak, however, the creature had pointed jaws that could be seen so clearly against the black background that one could even make out the tiny teeth, at least for a moment. But then the oxygen made everything dissolve, the fine lines blurred before the man's eyes, which made him giddy for an instant, and when he took off the second glove—he shook it away— and ran his finger over the remains of the image, it crumbled into dust. But for a moment he had felt something of its contours, the delicate talons, and received a quiet shock—the kind one experiences when one strokes the back of a letter with one's fingertips and can still feel the hand, the grip, of someone long dead.

He tied the scarf around his mouth, locked the chisel back into the hammer and cleared away the two cubic metres that were still necessary for him to break through.

Fattie wasn't there when I went to the animal club in the afternoon; there was no one sitting under the canopy or by the fireplace, and Zorro barked and scratched at the cardboard sheet when he heard me. The lock was stuck, as always; one had to pull the door towards oneself to turn the key, but that was impossible if the dog put its paws through the crack. I went around to the back of the old construction trailer, which was standing in the undergrowth without its wheels, pushed the little window open and threw in the parcel I had brought—fried potatoes wrapped in newspaper. Zorro barked, pounced on it growling and champing, and I quickly ran back to the door and unlocked it. The two wood pigeons in the upper cage gave a startled coo when the afternoon sun shone into the room, and Lümmel, the grey cockatiel on the perch under the ceiling, also opened his wrinkled eyelids. The guinea pig squeaked, and the rabbits ran excitedly through the hay as soon as I peeped over the edge of their box, which had a lid made of chicken wire. There were three; mine was the white one—Mister Sweet, whose ears looked transparent in the glaring light. One could see the veins.

Zorro ate up the fried potatoes, devouring them together with the softened paper as if he had not been fed for days. And yet there were still almond biscuits in his feeding bowl. The cockatiel had millet seeds, the pigeons had maize, there were carrots and cauliflower leaves in the rabbit cage, and the bowl for the cat on a

shelf next to the window was filled; the milk looked cur-
dled, though. Beside it lay a herring's head, black with
flies.

No messages to be found. There were candle
stumps everywhere, and on the floor, which we had
covered with a thick layer of cardboard, were stamped-
out cigarette butts and sweet wrappers. There were three
plastic carnations in a cracked glass won by Fattie at the
shooting stand during the last fair. It stood on top of
the supplies box I had fashioned together with the
Marondes, and I opened the lid and counted my *Sigurd
and Bodo* comics. Next to unripe ears of wheat, old
bread, a few magazines and empty bottles, there was also
a five-pack of Stuyvesant, and I took the broom and
swept the clubhouse. The dust swirled through the
broad sunbeam.

After Zorro had eaten the potatoes, he leapt up and
rolled about in front of me. I suppose he was a hunting
dog, greying with brown patches, but he had a hip
injury; I bent down and scratched his belly until the red
dwarf's cap appeared and he started biting my hand.
Not hard, more playfully, but he had sharp teeth. I
pushed him away, renewed the hay in the rabbit pen
and threw the fish head into the bushes. Then I sat

down in front of the hut, pulled my knife out of my pocket and carried on carving my new weapon, the spear. It was a young, dead straight alder trunk, and the head was made of a long roofing nail that I had laid on the tracks, under the freight train. A tip from old Pomrehn, who owned the property our hut stood on. He may have been a bit crazy, but he knew a lot of tricks.

I heard him hammering somewhere. The lilac and elder bushes grew so high here that all one could see of his house was the mossy roof with its sagging ridge; it was an old farmhouse with a cracked timber framework that lost a little more of its clay coat after every storm. The well in the courtyard was covered with a concrete slab, and if one moved the handle of the pump there was a gurgling sound, a squelching and slurping deep down, but water came out only rarely. And when it did, it was brown with rust.

Pomrehn had grown rapeseed and kept cows in the place where our housing estate stood; then his wife died, and he sold the land to the mining authorities, paid his bank debts and got himself a few shoemaker's machines. But as the shoes he repaired soon fell apart again, people soon stopped bringing them, and the workshop in what was once the living room fell into disrepair. There was a coat of fine leather dust on the machines and shelves, which still contained a pair of turquoise pumps and a single boot, and the old man sat in the kitchen all day, rolling himself a store of cigarettes and drinking beer and schnapps, usually Doornkaat.

But he was rarely alone. He let all the children from the neighbourhood into his house; they could romp around wherever they wanted, even in the marital bed, and it didn't bother him if they stole something. One time, Roswitha Vogel ran through the estate wearing a veil-cloaked hat, and in the sandpit behind the church there lay a silver cake slice with an ivory handle. Pomrehn liked children, and all the year round he collected the tiny Doornkaat bottles for them in a cardboard box under the stove. Then, if there was snow in the courtyard, he filled them with water, screwed on the lids and pushed them into the ash compartment, right under the grill. It was so hot there that it was better to put on the work gloves that lay in the coal scuttle.

Whoever bought beer, tobacco or tinned beans for him got them as a reward, and sometimes we also used them to shoot at cats; he didn't like them. He was convinced they had made his wife ill, that she had choked on cat hair, and he showed no mercy if he saw one approaching the house.

'That cat's done it's last shit! Give it some!' Then we rushed to the stove, opened the flap, sent the hot bottles flying out through the open window and watched them explode in the snow. A muffled, often delayed smashing sound accompanied by flying shards and earth. But we never hit a cat.

That had been the winter before, and he seemed to have become even skinnier since then. He was standing under the elder bushes holding a pipe wrench, and nodded at me. He had tied his corduroy trousers together with a piece of clothesline, and his grey vest was full of holes.

'Hey! Are you a cowboy or an Indian?' He asked all the boys that question, and I must have answered it about 10 times before that. He didn't like cowboys very much. I pointed at my spear.

'Blackfoot.'

'Of course, I forgot again. You're Tecumseh, right?' That was my name when we played Wild West, and I nodded and carried on carving away at my spear. When we played knights I was Sigurd. 'Everything is important for an Indian.' Pomrehn looked over the field towards the horizon. His chin was full of white stubble, and he had large eyes that always watered slightly. 'Every stone along the way, every cracked twig. You'll learn things you can use for your whole life, for example tracking. You've chosen attentiveness.' He took a step out of the shade. 'All cowboys do is shoot around . . . Nice spear you've got there.'

He wasn't wearing any shoes. His feet were red and blue with veins, and most of his toenails were ingrown. 'Where are your mates then?'

Zorro came out of the undergrowth with the fish head in his jaws, and I shrugged my shoulders. The old man sat down next to me and propped the wrench against the wall. He smelled a bit musty, like his house, and didn't seem to know where he should put his hands. First he put them on either side on the bench, then on his knees, then finally under his armpits. 'So who you fighting today?'

With my tongue between my teeth, I was trying to concentrate on the pattern, the snake. It was wound around the upper third, up to the head. 'Don't know. The whole Kleekamp gang's on holiday. Camping in Meinerzhagen.'

'Oh really? That can't be helped then. You'll just have to smoke a peace pipe. Do you ever smoke one?'

'Not really. Only rarely.'

He ran his fingers through his thin hair. 'And what do you put in it?'

'In what?'

'Well, in the pipe, the chillum. What tobacco?'

'We put tea in it. From teabags. Smokes too.'

'I see.'

In the clubhouse the rabbits were getting active. They must have been chasing each other around in circles; the pattering of their paws sounded as if the floor beneath them was hollow, and Pomrehn placed one leg over the other and folded his hands in front of his knee. But he moved them apart again immediately and scratched both forearms at the same time.

'Did you watch TV yesterday?' I shook my head. 'That was something, I tell you. Someone operated on himself. A case of life-threatening appendicitis in snowy Siberia, no doctor anywhere. So he took a kitchen knife and a mirror, and it was only when he was sewing the wound up again with cotton thread that he fainted. It's really true! Now what was it called . . .'

The snake's eye didn't turn out well. 'As Far As Your Feet Can Carry You.' I just mumbled, and he looked around, stretching his neck. 'Yes, that could be it . . . My word, it stinks like hell here. I don't suppose you boys've got anything to smoke in your hut? Maybe tobacco?'

'No. But I can go to the Kaldes' and buy you some.'

He sat upright and looked at me. 'Would you do that? And how am I going to pay for it?'

'Well, from your pension.'

He grinned bitterly. 'That's right. If I had one, my son. If I had one . . . But I'm not going crawling, not to them. I'm not standing around in offices at my age. They can all kiss my arse!' He took the spear out of my hands, examined the patterns and weighed it in his hands. 'Tea, you say? Tea works too?'

'Well, it makes plenty of smoke . . . but I don't know if one can really smoke it.'

He nodded and felt the tip with his thumb. Then I got a shock: Lilly, the tabby cat, a real colossus, was coming towards us through the grass—though at first one could only see the ears. She meowed quietly, her heavy belly wobbling with every step she took, and I was just about to clap my hands and shoo her away with a hiss. Then the old man looked up.

'Hey, who's that? New here?'

'No, no. She's in the animal club, has been for about a year. She's pregnant.'

He snorted, making a dry bogey in his nose leap out and shoot back in again. 'You don't say. Then she can't smoke, can she?' He propped up the spear against the hut, bent over and let his hand dangle from the bench. 'Come over here then, my little one.' Lilly took a few quicker steps, smelled the yellow fingers, rubbed her head against them, and he stroked her between the ears. She purred, rolled onto her side and started trampling with her front paws.

'Hey! I thought you hate cats!'

He shook his head. 'Oh no, not me. In fact, I rather like them. It's just my wife, she finds the little beasts terrible. Asthma.'

'Your wife? But she's dead, isn't she?'

With the back of his hand he stroked the light

belly, the rosy teats, and closed his eyes for a moment. 'Oh, my boy. What would you know . . .'

I stood up and took the spear into the hut. The guinea pig was squeaking, but I couldn't see it under the hay. It was probably afraid of the rabbits, which were still chasing each other, and the wood pigeons also cooed restlessly in their cage when my shadow fell on it. But the cockatiel was dozing, its beak slightly open; one could watch the tongue pulsating gently. Zorro was sleeping too.

Pomrehn raised his head and frowned when I handed him the Stuyvesant. 'That was still lying here.'

'Is that true? I'll be damned!' His hand trembled a little. 'Then we should bring it to safety right away, shouldn't we? All underage here.'

After he had taken out a cigarette, he put the pack in his pocket. He broke off the filter, lit the cigarette and leaned back against the wall of wooden boards with a sigh. The smoke wafted sluggishly over the grass and up into the trees. The sunbeams shone through the branches, there was already a touch of evening in the air, and while Pomrehn inhaled deeply and I cleaned my knife on the bench, we looked down silently at the cat. She lay at our feet in a shuddering patch of light, breathing calmly, and now and again she opened her bright eyes and looked up at us. Then it was like looking into the watery depths. The babies were moving under her fur.

It was hot that night. I couldn't fall asleep again after being woken by a sound, the slamming of a door somewhere in the house. My sister was allergic to mosquito bites: they often turned into real bumps, and because they gave her a fever, the windows had to stay closed at night. I pulled the curtain a bit to the side. The moon was almost full, and in the light I could see that Sophie was sweating too. The light hair clung a little more darkly to her temples, and there were tiny drops sparkling on her nose. But she was sleeping calmly with the yellow teddy in her arms. It only had one eye, and that one was hanging down a bit.

I sat down on the edge of the bed. The glass on my bedside table was empty, and for a moment I thought about whether I should drink from the watering-can behind the cactuses; the floorboards creaked, and I didn't want to wake Sophie. But then I went over my bed; it was just a step from the end to the door.

In the hall, which was tiny, hung my father's trousers. There were two bicycle clips attached to the hem of the right pocket. The floorboards in the living room also groaned, but here there were bridges, so it wasn't as loud. Big plants behind the curtains kept out the light from the street lamps, and in the furthest corner it was so dark that I could hardly see anything apart from the cold TV screen, the glimmer of the writing: Loewe-Opta. There were cigarettes and a lighter on the armrest of the couch, and as I was just about to go into the kitchen, I noticed that the front door was open by about an inch. I carefully pushed it shut.

The dishes on the dresser had been washed. Glasses and salad bowls sparkled in the moonlight, and I stood in front of the sideboard and looked across the garden, where the fences cast blue shadows, to Fernewaldstrasse. It was completely deserted. A fox trotted along under the lanterns towards the mine tower.

I pulled open the fridge and squatted down. In the door was a bottle of milk with a silver lid, and on the shelf were three boiled potatoes and a little bottle of

RALF ROTHMANN

Chicogo nail varnish. As well as a cube of margarine
and a few slices of sausage in greaseproof paper, and I
rolled one of them up, pushed it into my mouth and
devoured it, skin and all. There was no fizzy water or
raspberry syrup, and I was just about to shut the door
again. But then, on the bottom shelf, behind the packet
with sandwiches, I found my father's tea flask. It had a
rubber ring under the lid, the kind beer bottles used to
have, and the dented aluminium was covered in pearls
of condensation.

I pulled it out and held it against my forehead, the
back of my neck and the undersides of my arms. The
tea inside was so icy that I already had a headache after
two gulps; but it tasted delicious—black tea with sugar
and lemon—,and I sat down on the floor in front of the
open fridge and kept taking little sips. Drops of water
fell onto my gym shorts and vest, and when I let out a
single silent burp the breath on the back of my hand
felt almost as cold as the tea.

I kept on drinking, telling myself before each gulp
that it was the last one. But then I took another, then
another smaller one, groaning quietly, and finally the
bottle was empty; there was just a little bit left that gurgled inside when I held it up to my ear, and I stood up,

put in two spoonfuls of sugar, and filled it up with tap water. Then I put it back.

I looked through the closed balcony door and across the garden. The bushes and trees were paler than their shadows, and some of them looked like the out-lines of animals; others seemed to have faces with black eye sockets and shaggy eyebrows. Behind the Tszi-maneks' beans stood their new DKW. Nobody in sight. Only the fox was still on Fernewaldstrasse, probably a young one. It went onto its hind legs and snapped after the mosquitoes and moths dancing in the light of the street lamps. Sometimes it even jumped.

I went back into the hall, heard a rustling in my parents' room and held my breath, watching the crack under the door. It stayed black. The only light was in the bathroom. My sister had probably left it on. The switch next to the mirror was too high for her, and usu-ally she couldn't be bothered to climb onto the little stool she stood on to brush her teeth once she had peed. I cleared my throat. The door wasn't locked, and when I crossed the threshold the handle slipped out of my sweaty hand.

'Keep quiet!'

I hadn't said anything. I just stared. She was wearing a light blue T-shirt and standing in front of the toilet with her legs as far apart as her knickers, which had slipped down to her knees, allowed. Her skin was the colour of caramel, with a delicate gleam; she went almost every day to Alsbachtal, the only swimming pool near us. But in the place where her bikini bottoms normally were, Marusha was white, and the dense layer of little hairs on her skin was as shiny as a mole's fur. She stood motionless, looking at me as if she were waiting for me to leave. She was holding something between her muscular legs, maybe a cloth or some cotton wool, and I quickly pulled the door shut.

Went back to the kitchen. The fox was gone, and I stood on tiptoe and peed in the sink. In Marusha's room there was a chamber pot with lid that she took downstairs with her in the mornings. As far as I knew, she had never used our toilet before, though my mother had allowed it 'in emergencies . . .' That was why the front door was never locked. I turned on the tap and gave a quick rinse.

There was an alarm clock on top of the wall cupboard. My father would be getting up in an hour to get ready for his shift, and I opened the fridge, turned up the cooling and took another slice of sausage. But as I held it in my hand, I suddenly had to burp. The tea went up my nose with a sour taste, and I put the sausage back and closed the door.

I wasn't tired at all now. I heard the sound of flush-ing, and Marusha came out of the bathroom; she didn't care about the creaking floorboards. She plodded straight to the door, and I gave a quiet 'Sshh!' Now she was the one who got a shock, laid one hand on her breastbone and closed her eyes for a moment. I had the moonlight behind me and could see the sanitary towel through her knickers, pure and white.

'Do you have to give me such a shock!' That wasn't even a whisper, almost just a breath, and I grinned.

'Are you injured?'

She scratched the back of her neck. 'Am I what? Go to bed, sunshine. The night's almost over.'

'Why should I?' I leaned against the frame of the kitchen door and crossed my arms. 'It's the holidays.'

'Maybe for you.' She yawned. 'But I've got a job interview tomorrow. At Kaiser und Gantz.'

'In Sterkrade? What you going to do there? Sell curtains?'

She didn't answer, instead pointing to the sofa arm-rest, to the packet of cigarettes. 'D'you suppose I can take one?'

I shrugged my shoulders. 'They're my father's. No filter.'

'So what? You think I'll wet myself?'

'Nah. You already have.'

She brushed one of her curls back behind her ear, and in the moonlight her smile seemed even more ra-diant than usual. 'Have what?' Then she knocked a Gold-Dollar out of the packet. 'You know, you may be pretty, but you're a bit funny in the head, aren't you?' She stepped into the hall and motioned with her head. 'Come on, let's have a chinwag.'

I pushed myself off from the doorframe. 'What do you mean, I'm pretty?'

But she didn't answer, and disappeared into her room. I had never been inside, only seen it from our balcony. Although one side of the window was open, there was a sweetish smell, like sweaty bedclothes. One of the legs of the life-size Graham Bonney cut-out hadn't been stuck on yet, and there was a recorder lying on the small shelf with Enid Blyton books; there was hardly any gloss left on the mouthpiece. On the carpet in front of the wardrobe stood her new record player, a portable battery-powered one with a slit to push singles in. A few of them were lying on the floor: 'She Loves You', 'Marmor, Stein und Eisen', 'Poor Boy'. Marusha sat down on the old bed.

She pulled up the cover around her hips and leaned against the back wall, which had fruits carved into it—apples and grapes. Then she smelled the cigarette, lit it and spat out a tobacco crumb before blowing the smoke out of her mouth. I went to the small desk, which had a dozen passport photos lying on it. She had spots on some of them.

'So when are you moving out?'

She looked at the glowing end, frowning. 'I was expecting it to be stronger. What a joke . . . What did you say? Why move out?'

'Well, if you're working now . . . Then you can afford a place of your own, can't you?'

'Are you crazy? As a trainee?'

'Or move in with your boyfriend.'

'What boyfriend?'

'Well, the guy with the Kreidler.'

'Jonny?!' She let out a grunt. 'You've got some funny ideas. I wouldn't even let him lick my feet. Or do you like him?'

'Don't know. No. Likes to get into fights, doesn't he.'

'True.' She was watching the cigarette smoke, the cloud under the lamp. 'He's strong.'

'But he's not your type at all. He's got those scars.'

'Where? Oh, you mean the one on the chin? Well . . . I don't think scars are bad at all on men. They look interesting.'

'I don't think they do. My father's got scars all over. From the war and rockfalls in the mine. All the coal dust went into the skin. If I had something like that—I'd have an operation.'

She closed her eyes for a moment, and her smile looked somehow understanding. There was a tiny down feather hanging in her hair. 'So is your mother going to hospital now?'

I shrugged my shoulders and sat down on the chair. 'No idea. I hope not. Then I'd have to look after my sister all day long.'

'So what? Little girls are sweet. The way they tag along.' She blew the smoke out through her nose and brushed off the ash on the edge of the old baby cream tin under the lamp on the bedside table. There was a half-sucked sweet inside. 'And you'd have the place to yourself, you could invite your mates, your girlfriend . . .'

'Who?' I pulled my feet up onto the seat and wrapped my arms around my knees. 'Are you joking? I haven't got a girlfriend! I'm 12.'

She nodded. There were a few fingernail cuttings stuck to the sweet. 'But you've started wanking, haven't you?'

A feeling came over my face as if my tongue were being held against a battery, and Marusha grinned. 'Oh God, what have I said now! You're blushing!'

'No I'm not.' The words somehow got stuck in my throat. I didn't feel like talking about things like that, and pretended I had to yawn. Marusha leaned her head back and blew a few perfect, ever smaller smoke rings upwards.

'Don't let me spoil you . . . Hey, what's up with your mother? What's her problem?'

'What do you mean, what's up? Gall bladder!'

'I know that. I mean why does she hit you all the time? Do you get up to so much trouble? You're a good boy, aren't you?'

'No idea. She doesn't hit me that often.'

'Yeah, right! You think I don't hear it? Nearly every week. She breaks wooden spoons beating you kids.'

'Rubbish! Not Sophie, she's still little. Anyway, sometimes I do stupid stuff. Things like running away from school. And if I'm dirty . . .'

'But that's no reason to beat a child!'

'So what? Don't you cop anything? Your father's given you a smack too.'

'What father? I don't have a father.'

'Well, Gorny then. When you wanted to go to church in a short skirt.'

'That's my business. And if he lays another finger on me, I'll tell Jonny. Then he'll pick him up from the mine.' She had leaned back into the corner with a pillow behind her neck, and stretched out an arm to offer me the rest of the cigarette. 'I'm turning 16. I don't have to take anything from him! Do you think you could . . . ?' She licked her lips. 'Tastes like straw.'

I stood up and put out the cigarette on the tin lid. She took off her friendship rings, four of them, and placed them on the windowsill. Then she stretched, yawned, and I went up to the bed and showed her the wound on the ball of my thumb, which was slowly healing. 'Look. That'll be a scar too.'

She grinned and took my hand. Her fingers were warm, but dry, and as she leaned forward I could look into her T-shirt, at the golden anchor hanging between her breasts on a thin chain. 'That's not a scar, sunshine. More like a scratch!'

I gulped. 'But it will be.'

My arm began to shake. She wasn't holding me tightly, but didn't really let me go either, stroking my palm with her fingertips, very softly, as if she were just stirring air. She looked me in the eyes, smiling. 'You're going red again. Do you like that?'

I shook my head and moved back, maybe a bit too abruptly. The bedside rug slipped and I stepped on a record, something by Udo Jürgens. 'Oh, shit! I didn't mean to do that. Sorry.'

'Doesn't matter.' She sank back down onto her pillow. 'It's your mother's anyway.'

I bent down to pick it up, and stayed there for a few moments to hide my erection. We only had three records on our phonograph: one by Chris Howland, one by Rita Pavlone and one by Billy Mo. I didn't know this one. 'Oh, it's new. She must have brought it back from town. Any good?'

'Don't know. It's okay. You can have it back.' She pulled the thin cover up to her chin, but stretched both legs out from under it, and I looked at her toes, the dark varnish. In some places she had got some on her skin too.

'What for? If Mum lent it to you, I'm sure you can keep it a bit longer.'

Marusha yawned deeply; it sounded like a cat hissing. 'She didn't lend it to me.' Then she closed her eyes and turned to the wall. 'I borrowed it. Turn off the light when you go out, okay?'

A cherry stone in an empty jam jar. Roses carved into the butter with a warm teaspoon. There were cups and saucers on the table, the re-heated rolls had already cooled off again, and I leafed through my copy of the

The Leatherstocking Tales. Everyone was finished except Sophie; she still had her boiled egg in front of her. With her little nose curled up, she was trying to break through the elastic white with her spoon, and my mother was watching her. My father leaned back and took a sip of coffee. He was still wearing his pyjama trousers and a fresh vest that was very tight around the chest, and picked a few crumbs from the couch. His big hands were also covered in scars and scratches, and the fingernails looked jagged.

'I'm not a fool!' He looked at my mother. 'What do they think? The head foreman has trouble with the wife and takes it out on the deputy, who goes off and grabs the pit foreman, cuts his holidays, and then the pit foreman goes to the shifter and gives him shit for leaving out props. And of course he passes it on to the shaft supervisor!' He shook his head. 'I'm not having it. Listen, I told Motzkat, they're crazy. How am I supposed to use the plough with the contracts we've made? The miners'll laugh in my face. There's still some damming up to be done, and the upper routing's been installed without any support plate. So I say the chain conveyor has to be shortened—how else are we going to get any further into the seam?! Either the clearers get their material out, or someone finally teaches them how to stack properly!'

My mother, nodding now and again, lit a cigarette. But she kept her eyes on Sophie. She had cut through the egg white; much too far. The yolk dribbled onto the plate, and she spread it about with her finger, painting a face.

'And Motzkat says to me: "Of course, Walter, you're right. But you know that arse. He sits up there in front of his drawing-board and thinks coal grows at right angles."—"So fuck him," I say. "You're the foreman! We've broken through the hanging wall. Distance between the pre-drill caps one metre 50. So put the props under, and there we are. When a chain conveyor's lying on top of coal, the stall has to be cut out properly, otherwise the whole lot comes crashing down!" But do you think I heard anything from the top? Not a word.'

'I can imagine. You're probably just too thorough for them . . .' My mother flashed her eyes at Sophie, but she didn't notice. She dipped one corner of her jam roll in the yolk.

' "We need a duster," I say, "to sort out the barriers. There has to be a dust box put up every 25 metres, that's obvious."—"You're telling me," says Motzkat, "if I only had foremen like you, there'd be some order in this pigsty. But I have to use anyone who's available for drilling." These blockheads are enough to drive you crazy. No head drift, you understand, no hydraulic station, and me alone with some trainee hewer. It's enough to give you a rash.'

'I can believe that.' My mother reached across the table and pulled the plate away from Sophie. 'And you can stop making such a mess. What do you think you're doing?'

Sophie looked up in amazement. 'But I haven't finished eating!'

My mother didn't answer. With her right elbow resting on her left hand, she held her cigarette next to her face and looked at my father as if listening to him. He pulled a bit of skin off his thumbnail.

'And then I'm supposed to keep a record of the gas level as well.' He shook his head. 'A whole coal layer fell across the conveyor and buried Hübner. You know, that little fat guy from the pit party. The one who wanted to dance with you. The lift wasn't working, and we hauled the man nearly two miles on a ladder, all the way to the shaft. Can you imagine that? And then the deputy foreman opens the cage and asks me for the gas measurements! I say: "What? Now? Can't you see we've got an injured man here? You want him to croak it?!" I should have given him . . .'

He clicked his tongue quietly and Sophie nestled up to him. She lifted his arm, so that for a moment one could see the number tattooed there, and laid it around her neck. Then she stuck her tongue out at me.

'The left hand doesn't know what the right hand's doing over there. Of course you have to watch out when you're blasting at the split in the seam, to make sure nothing happens. And the blaster gawks at me as if I was barmy. One or two blasts to loosen up the rock under the coal, that's simple enough. Then the plough can drive through, and we'll pull the chain along with the heavy toolboxes on our backs. I tell you . . .'

He reached for my mother's packet, put a Chester between his lips, and she looked around for some matches. But Sophie already had the book in her hands and gave him a light. He stroked her head.

'But Motzkat is much too good-natured. He's the only foreman in the pit who doesn't mind getting his hands dirty. So I say: "Take a look at that, none of the props have been mortised; how am I supposed to expand anything here?" And what does he do? Gets out a saw and cuts me two dozen roundwoods! That's what he's like. And then this head foreman comes toddling out of his perfumed office and yells: "That's enough! You'll never reach your target like that! You have to get everyone who's available to pre-drill as long as it takes until the coal shift takes over the job for them." I almost hit the roof—"What? What coal shift?" I asked. "Who else is supposed to come? *We're* the coal shift!" You should have seen his face!'

'I can imagine. I wouldn't put up with it either.' My mother put out her cigarette in the eggshell. At the same time she put the glass lid on the butter dish. 'Do you want pasta or dumplings with your goulash? Or should I . . .'

'Dumplings!' Sophie almost screamed. Then she beamed at me. But my mother's face took on a sour expression.

'Typical. As always, madam chooses the thing that's the most work.'

'But you asked!'

My father gave a snort. 'Oh well, what's the use.'

RALF ROTHMANN

He stared in front of him. 'In this pit everyone does what they want. And the works committee's useless. Next week we have to go down to the lowest level, up to our arses in water. And there's a coffin lid hanging in the coal face . . . God! One shouldn't really let anyone in there. If it falls down—then good night.'

I wet my fingertip with my mouth and picked up a few crumbs from the table. Poppy seeds too. 'What's a coffin lid?'

My mother pulled out the tray behind her armchair and started putting the dishes on it. He passed her his eggcup. 'A stone block that's surrounded by splits and crevasses, so not really fixed. Some of them are huge, as big as a house, and when there's a lot of movement down there through the coal extraction, one of those things sometimes comes smashing down. Then you can hear the glasses shake in the cupboard here.'

'Walter!' My mother shook her head. 'Now don't go scaring the children. That sounds like war!'

He frowned. 'What? Why? What's that got to do with it?' The muscles in his right arm twitched as he put out his cigarette; he had hardly smoked any of it. At the same time, he blew the smoke down his chest. 'What a load of rubbish . . . I should know better what war is, shouldn't I?'

He leaned back again and made a sound as if he had something stuck between his teeth. His dark blonde hair was longer than usual, and had started curling up above his ears. Sophie looked up to him, fingering the dimple in his chin. 'Will there be war again soon, Dad?'

He gave a quick shake of the head, then reached for the Sunday paper. When I clicked my fingers he passed the page with the picture puzzle across the table to me, and my sister slid down from the couch and pulled her suitcase out from under it. It was full of Mickey Mouse comics. She took one out and sat down again. But didn't open it.

'Dad?' She wrapped a curl around her thumb. 'If there's war, will we have to shoot people dead?'

'Not you.' I grinned. 'You're short-sighted.'

But she didn't pay any attention to me. My father was reading the sports section, and she nudged him.

'Come on, tell us. Did you shoot in the war?'

He nodded. 'Sure. Everyone shot.'

'Properly? Did you shoot anyone dead?'

He didn't answer. But my mother, who was just coming out of the kitchen with a sponge to wipe the table, lifted a threatening finger at her. 'Sophie! What's all this about?' It sounded strict, but she was smiling as she said it, so my sister wasn't scared.

'Come on, Dad! Did you kill anyone?'

He breathed deeply, almost sighing, but didn't look up. His cheekbones twitched.

'Dad, please! Did they scream? Did they fall over properly, like on TV? Tell us!'

My mother stood still, as if also waiting for an answer. I crossed my arms, and he cleared his throat, lifted his head and reached for his cup. The white in his eyes looked completely pure.

Sophie was jumping about the couch on her knees. 'Come on Dad, please tell us! Did you shoot anyone dead? With blood and everything?'

My father was holding his cup without drinking from it. His hand was too big for the dainty little thing; his finger didn't fit through the handle. But his face suddenly seemed much softer. His eyebrows were slanted above his eyes, and he looked up to my mother and spoke in a strangely muted voice, as if we weren't in the room: 'What am I supposed to say now?'

She lifted her chin abruptly and came around the table, her heels clicking against the floor. 'Enough hopping around!' She gave me the sponge, which was dripping slightly, and grabbed my sister by the arm. 'Off to your room! Clear up the toy cupboard!'

The stove in our kitchen was white, an enamel monster full of baking and warming compartments. It was decorated with chrome handles and had a polished rail going around it, and there was a little trolley for wood and coal that one had to pull out from between the feet. They looked like cast-iron paws, and my mother cooked everything, even the eggs for breakfast, right on the embers. She managed to use the hooks, lids and iron rings like a blacksmith without ruining her freshly varnished nails.

I took the coal scuttles she had laid by the front door for me and went to the cellar. There was a sweet smell on the stairs, and the light, the neon lamp, was still broken. The Gornys' doors, all closed, had been constructed from roof beams, and through the cracks one could see shelves full of preserves—jars with apples, pears and beans. But also liver sausage and jellied meat.

Behind hoes and spades stood the scratched-up accordion case.

I whistled silently to myself. Our door at the end of the corridor, opposite the laundry room, had a padlock, but we didn't use it. The door was coated in linoleum, and I pushed it open with my shoulder, but left the light off. The coal pile was sparkling in the corner; some of the pieces had fool's gold on them. In the winter it had come up to my forehead, but now it wasn't even knee-high; one could tell by the soot-marks on the wall. I turned round.

'Don't get a shock . . . !'

Behind the tool shelf, half covered by the dust-stained sunlight shining at an angle through the small window, stood Herr Gorny. I was almost in the room now, and took a step back with my containers. They banged against the door. With his hands folded behind the front flap of his dungarees, he looked at me from the corner of his eye. The shadow of his bent nose fell across one half of his face, and his blue eyes were as bright as glass.

'I'm just looking for a repair kit. Do you know where I can find one?'

I didn't say anything, shook my head, and he came out of the shadows and pushed me with the back of his hand.

'Hey! Close your mouth. Milk teeth go sour. So what does your father use to fix his bike?'

'What? A repair kit, I think.'

'Well then. And where does he keep it?'

'Over there.' I motioned towards the other corner with my head, and Herr Gorny went to the old kitchen cabinet and pulled out the drawer. He was wearing heavy working shoes, but no shirt or vest, and I could smell his sweat. One of his braces slipped off the naked shoulder when he placed his fists on his hips.

'God, what a mess. How am I supposed to find anything here?' He had hair on his upper arms, but only on the back.

'On the left. Under the sandpaper.'

The old tobacco tin he pulled out and gave a quick shake contained the spare valves and the small plate for scraping away at the rubber tubing, which now rattled about inside it. He took off the lid.

'Aren't you here to get coal?' He pointed to the pile with the tube of glue. 'So don't let me stop you, boy.'

I bent down and pushed the coal scuttle across the stone floor. My father always filled it with a single movement, but I had to repeat the action several times, suppressing a groan. Herr Gorny was still standing behind me. When the first one was full, I put it to one side. He held the other one out to me and smiled thinly. 'You're doing it wrong, you know. That'll just tire you out. You have to push forwards, not down.'

The black tin of the coal scuttle already had holes in it. The sun shone through them, a very delicate spray of light, and I nodded, even though I didn't know what he meant. I pushed the opening into the coal.

'Good God, no! That's exactly how you shouldn't do it! Fold back the handle and then push. With the ball of your thumb. It's really simple.'

He put away the repair kit, bent down over me and took hold of my fingers, keeping a tight grip on them. The edges of his braces hanging down from the front flap of his dungarees tickled the back of my neck. 'Like that . . . Give it some elbow grease! You see.' One push and the rectangular bucket was full, but my knees were trembling from the effort of trying not to fall onto the coal. I inhaled Herr Gorny's breath.

'There you go, that wasn't so hard!'

When we stood up he let go of the handle, and the sudden weight pulled me to one side. For a moment I felt his shoulder against my ear, the naked skin. His gaze wandered down me again, and he grinned mockingly. 'But you're still young, aren't you. With strong calves like those, you'll get some decent muscles too. What d'you want to be when you grow up?'

I shrugged. 'Don't know. Maybe a miner? Like my father.'

'Oh, come on . . .' He straightened his braces. Then he took the tin and left the room. 'Don't be stupid!'

He left the wooden door open. But I still decided to put back some of the coal; the buckets would have been too heavy for me otherwise. Then I closed the drawer, and when I stepped into the corridor I saw Herr Gorny kneeling in the laundry room and submerging a pumped-up inner tube in a basin full of water. There was a ladies' bike leaning against the wall behind him.

'Julian?' He didn't look up from his work. 'I forgot to tell you: there are toys lying around all over the footpath. Those little cars of yours. Can you please clear them away? Someone could have a nasty fall if they step on one. And that'll cost a packet. Doesn't anyone teach you to be tidy?'

'Yes, sure. But the cars aren't mine. Not anymore. I gave them to little Schulz.'

Now he looked up. 'What? You gave away all your Matchbox cars? Why?'

'Well . . . No idea. I just did.'

'But there were a lot of them, weren't there? A real collection. And you just gave them away? Have you people got too much money?'

I grinned. 'No, we haven't. They were pretty old, you know. I covered up the scratches on the fire engines with nail varnish.'

'Aha.' He shut one eye. 'I suppose you like little Schulz?'

'Who? Oh . . . he's okay. He never cheats when we play cards. And he's always in a good mood.'

Herr Gorny nodded. 'A pretty boy, one has to admit.' He pushed down a new piece of tubing, turning it round and round. It creaked in his fists, and when he put his fingers in the water they seemed twice as thick. 'I bet he'll end up gay,' he added quietly, and frowned as a few bubbles rose to the surface.

It was already getting dark, and I rang the doorbell. Herr and Frau Kalde sold almost everything one could get at a kiosk at the top of their staircase. Even women's stockings. There was a board jammed between the ribs of their front door—that was the shop counter—and behind it stood fridges, freezers and shelves. On the fuse box a glass full of Knöterich boiled sweets; one got those if the change was only one or two pfennigs, though it was always more with us.

The hallway was tiled up to shoulder height. The two customers there—Frau Breuers, who was just being given a net full of bottles and a five mark note, and Herr Kwehr, who was taking an ice cream cone out of its wrapping paper, strawberry ice cream—turned round. It seemed as if they had just been laughing about something—their faces looked relaxed—and I nodded to them before stepping up to the board.

'One says "Good evening"!' Frau Breuers looked me up and down. She was wearing a sleeveless nylon overall, dark blue, and her upper arms were as thick as my legs. 'Good grief! What holes have you been messing around in? Your mother'll be very happy about that, won't she?'

I had a crease in my trouser leg and was covered in ash and grass. Herr Kwehr turned up his nose and sniffed loudly. 'You think he's already messing around in holes?'

Frau Breuers's little eyes opened wide. She opened her mouth so wide that one could see the gap between her teeth on one side, then took a breath theatrically. 'Wilfried! Really . . . You're lucky you're not my husband. I'd show you a thing or two!'

Herr Kwehr licked some ice cream off his thumb and dropped the gold paper into the bucket in the corner. 'Well, I should hope so. As your husband, I'd finally have a right to see it, wouldn't I?' She screeched. It echoed through the hall, and she quickly put her hand over her mouth, the one with the money in it. She had red spots on her neck.

Frau Kalde never smiled. She wore glasses that magnified her eyes enormously, and the corners of her wide lips always hung down; a bit lower with children than with adults. 'So?' She stuck out her chin. 'What do *you* want then?' I could see the fingerprints on her thick lenses and turned my head a bit. The neighbours, who had been whispering behind my back, still seemed to want to stay, and looked at me curiously again.

'The usual, please.'

Frau Kalde frowned. 'And what's that supposed to be?'

I cleared my throat. 'Well, two packets of Chester, one packet of Gold-Dollar, and two bottles of beer.'

'There, you see!' Herr Kwehr bit into his ice cream, the chocolate coating. 'He'll be out on the town tonight. He knows how to get the girls on side.'

'Wait a minute . . .' Frau Kalde turned round, eyeing her shelf. 'Didn't your sister just buy that?' She pushed the curtain that covered the apartment entrance slightly to one side. 'Horst?'

Her husband didn't answer. All one could hear was quiet music, a brass band, and I stepped closer to the counter. 'I don't know anything about that. My mother said I should bring those things with me when I come home this evening.'

'Horst? My goodness, where's he got to!'

Frau Breuers nodded. 'You can't let these men out of your sight for a moment . . . I'll be off then.'

'Horst!' thundered Frau Kalde. 'Are you in the cellar?!'

'Don't worry, it's okay. Maybe my sister really was here. I'll ask first and then come back.'

She shook her head. 'Must be in the cellar . . .' Then she put two bottles of beer on the board, Ritter Export, warm. But she knew my father only drank DAB. Still, I kept quiet. She put the cigarettes next to them, took the pencil out of her apron pocket and added everything together. 'Empties?' I told her I didn't have any, and she ran her tongue across her teeth. 'That'll be four marks thirty, please.'

Herr Kwehr gave a quiet whistle and Frau Breuers puffed out her cheeks. 'My God! I'm glad none of us smokes. Not cheap, is it!'

Frau Kalde looked at me expectantly. She knew what I would say, and could just as easily have reached behind for the account book, a grey notebook. But she wanted to hear it, again and again, and especially if there were other customers standing in the hall. I gulped and scratched the back of my neck. 'On the tab please.'

The woman reached for the door lintel, where there was a single spider's thread, and pulled it away. 'What did you say?' Then she quickly looked over to the others, and for a second it looked as if her eyes were rolling about uncontrollably behind her glasses. 'You'll have to speak up if you want me to understand what you're saying. We're not in church.'

Frau Breuers bit off a piece of the ice cream cone that Herr Kwehr was holding out to her and licked her lip. 'On the tab please,' I repeated, putting the cigarettes in my pockets; I loved fingering new packets. Then I took the bottles from the board and went to the door, opening it with my elbow. The neighbours started whispering behind me, but Frau Kalde answered them normally, without lowering her voice at all. She took down the sum in the exercise book.

'Oh no, she only comes when she's got cash. She's ashamed to buy on credit—she sends the children to do that.'

I stepped out, and the door fell shut. At the end of the street where the wasteland began, the Marondes were playing soccer with half a briquette, and Fattie was sitting in the grass, holding one of his Wild West stories up close to his eyes. He had folded it so that he could read one column at a time. He moved his lips while he read. His real name was Olaf, and he didn't like it at all when we called him Fattie. He wasn't really fat either, just bigger and stronger than we were, and already 15. He rode his brother's Zündapp Bella through the estate without a moped licence, and even the boys from the Kleekamp gang respected him. I put everything down on the kerb, and he whistled through his teeth.

'Well well! You won the lottery?'

'No. But I couldn't buy Stuyvesant, especially not a five pack. They would have smelled a rat. It's supposed to be for my parents, you see?'

He nodded, but frowned. The briquette slid against a fencing post and shattered. Karl slapped me on the back, bent down to get a bottle, and took off the crown cap with his teeth. Froth poured out, and his brother eyed the cigarettes and smelled the packets. I put my hands behind my belt and pulled my shoulders up slightly. 'Am I in the club again?'

Fattie stood up. His hair was reddish at the tips from the late sun, but I could only see dark cavities where his eyes were. The Marondes were somewhere be-hind me, and in the twilight I couldn't see his grin, only sense it; but it was there, like a cool streak in the air, and suddenly he gave me a push with his lower body—but not hard enough to knock me over. I just took a

step back, or tried to. But then Franz was on all fours behind me, so I fell down after all. Karl laughed dirtily as
I lay in the grass, pocketed the cigarettes, and I repeated
my question.

'Of course.' Fattie's voice came out of the darkness
and he opened his beer. 'You're always welcome.'

The next day, after the early shift was over, I went some
of the way to meet my father as he came. He didn't
really like that, not anymore, and this time too, he
twisted his mouth when he saw me standing at the edge
of Dorstener Strasse and gave a quick shake of his head.
One of the other miners cycling along next to him
grinned. One of the others called out something to me
that I didn't understand; the Laakenot trucks that
picked up the slag from the mine by the piece were too
loud. We called them cat death.

My father stopped and put his folded-up corduroy
jacket on the carrier. 'What's for lunch?'

I sat down and put my feet on the wing nuts. 'Fried
potatoes with fried eggs and spinach.' Then I wrapped
my arms around his hips and put my cheek against his

back. I could smell the curd soap he washed himself with in the coop through his flannel shirt, and he started pedalling.

'Come on, why are you sitting like that? You're not a girl. Hold on to the saddle!'

I sat up, put my fingertips under the leather edge, and he turned off the road and took the path between the fields, which was very uneven. The mudguards rattled, and when I stuck out a leg I could brush against the ears of wheat. The carrier left a waffle-print on my bottom.

When we got home, I took the bag off the handle-bars and went up the stairs whistling. The steps were freshly polished, gleamed in the sun, and I took off my sandals and called my mother through the half-opened door. But she didn't answer, and for a moment I stayed in the doorway. I couldn't smell any onions or bacon, and the living room table wasn't set either. The radio wasn't on, and in the kitchen there were potatoes, a piece of margarine and a block of spinach in a puddle of water on the dresser; but nothing in the oven except ashes.

Not a sound. No one in the bedroom either; the bedspread lay neatly folded on the bed and the metal alarm clock was ticking. A solitary fly scurried across the fringe of the lampshade, and I called again and knocked on the bathroom door. But it had been left ajar. The narrow window was open, and there were nylon stockings lying unwashed in the bath; every time a drop of water fell onto the lightly-coloured heap, it moved. Next to the soap dish lay a little tube of painkillers, slightly squashed; the screw top lay on the floor.

I heard my father coming up the stairs with slow, heavy steps, went onto the balcony and looked out to the garden. 'Lollypop? Where's Mum?'

Sophie was sitting alone on the edge of the sand-box. One of her teddies was buried up to its neck, and she looked up. Although the sun was behind her, she covered her eyes with her hand. 'I'm not hungry.'

My father, who had heard the question, went to the kitchen and looked around. 'Why? Where would she be?'

I shrugged. 'Maybe in the cellar. Hanging up laundry? Shall I have a look?' But he didn't answer. He threw his jacket on the sofa and called her; his voice was strangely muted. The glasses in the cabinet trembled slightly as he walked across the floorboards. In the bathroom he bent down to pick up the lid and screwed it back on the tube of tablets. Then he pushed open the door of the children's room and placed his hands on his hips. His broad back blocked my view.

'What's going on?' His voice sounded amazed, and I pushed past him. Our room was full of smoke, and my mother, slightly bent forward, was lying in Sophie's bed. Although she was wearing her quilted dressing gown, she had pulled the cover, the one decorated with toadstools and dwarves, up to her chest, and didn't look at us. Her head was turned to the wall, her eyes closed, and she was holding an extinguished cigarette between her fingers. There were tears, grey with eyeliner, on Sophie's pillow.

I bent down over her. 'What's the matter? Did you have another colic?'

She sniffled quietly, but didn't say anything. Her foot, which was poking out of the end of the covers, still had one of the slippers with the plush edging on it. She was wearing her pearl necklace, and I pulled the cigarette butt out from between her fingers and threw it into the bowl on the bedside rug. My father breathed out sharply through his nose and ran both his hands through his hair.

'Shall we call you an ambulance?'

She swallowed hard, again and again, as if she had something stuck in her throat. 'What's the point.' She spoke quietly, almost in a whisper, and hardly moved her mouth. 'Just let me lie here.'

My father shrugged his shoulders. He turned round and went into the kitchen, and while I took the slippers off her feet and placed them next to the bed I could hear him tinkering with the stove rings and scratching about in the coal scuttle; it was much louder than when she did it. I bent down and brushed a strand of hair from her forehead. Her skin felt dull from the spray.

'Shall I make a hot water bottle?' She nodded almost invisibly. Her eyelids were trembling, and I turned round to go to the bathroom—and found my father standing in the doorway again. Folds going down over the bridge of his nose. His lips so pale that I could hardly make them out from the rest of his skin, he held the half-thawed packet of spinach in his fist like a brick.

'Now listen here . . .' He went up close to the little bed. 'If you're not feeling well, please go to the doctor. And if there's something wrong with your gall bladder, it's about time you had an operation. What are hospitals for? I'm getting sick and tired of all this back and forth. When I come out of that hole where I work myself half to death for you all every day, I expect to have something to eat, you understand! Then I bloody well expect to see some food on the table!'

He was speaking more loudly than I had ever heard him speak before, and when he screamed 'Do you understand me!' after that, I saw his lower row of teeth, the brown in the gaps between them. With a kick, he sent the ashtray next to the bed flying into the corner.

But it stayed in one piece, even though it was made of glass. But the five cigarette butts inside it jumped onto the carpet. 'And now get the hell up! If you can smoke one fag after another, you can make your family something to eat!'

He turned round and went back to the kitchen, his heels banging on the floorboards, and my mother laid an arm across her eyes. But the shimmering fabric of her dressing gown didn't soak up the tears. They ran down under her sleeve, and I went to the corner and picked up the cigarette butts, then put them back in the bowl.

When I woke up, I saw that one corner of my bird poster had come off the wall. The drawing-pin was lying on the bed. I pushed the curtain to the side and opened the window. A few white clouds in the sky, as delicate as fluff, and a freight train whistling somewhere behind Fernewaldstrasse. But one couldn't see it.

Sophie had already got up. She was sitting at the balcony table and pushing one of my circus animals, a tiger with long-faded stripes, through a plate of Honey Pops. 'Julian!' She beamed at me. 'Shall I make you breakfast?'

I shook my head, took the cornflakes out of the cupboard and poured them onto my plate. It had a locomotive pattern on it. The sun still wasn't very high, there was dew sparkling in the grass under the trees, and there were several pairs of nylon stockings hanging on the clothesline. They were moving gently in the wind.

'Where's Mum? At the doctor's?'

'No, I don't think so. You know what? I've got a big secret. But I can't tell you.'

I sat down at the table and dug my spoon into the sugar bowl. 'Of course not, or it wouldn't be a secret. Where are your glasses?'

'I can see enough.'

'You can now. But one day you'll be blind or have a squint. Then none of the men will want you. So, where's Mum? Shopping?'

'I'll tell you.' She leaned forwards, cupped her hands around her mouth like a funnel and whispered: 'She's picking our baby up!'

'What did you say?!'

My sister nodded solemnly. 'Oh yes. We're having a baby.'

'Rubbish! How's that supposed to happen! She'd have had to be pregnant first, wouldn't she?'

Sophie grunted. The rubber tiger was lying in the milk, and she navigated around it with her spoon to fish out the last Honey Pops. 'We're only borrowing it. From Frau Gimbel. Because she has to go to a funeral.'

'Oh, so you mean Mum has to look after it. What a great secret. Wow, amazing!'

Sophie shook her head. There was a little ladybird stuck on the clasp holding back a lock of hair above her forehead. 'No! *That's* not the secret. It's much, much nicer.'

'Why are you whispering?' I looked through the open window in Marusha's room. 'There's no one here.'

The bed was unmade, and there was a Klingel fashion catalogue lying on the floor. There were clothes hangers dangling from the wardrobe, the washbasin and even the lamp; they were all empty.

My sister reached under the table and scratched her knee. 'Julian? Is it true that I'm from the milkman?'

'That you're what? Why? Where d'you get silly ideas like that?'

'Wolfgang said so. Redheads are from the milkman.'

'Don't be stupid! Firstly you hair isn't red, more like strawberry blonde. And then you're from Dad, just like me. I'll smash his face in, that Gorny arsehole.'

'Well, you're not that strong. Anyway, I don't care if I'm from the milkman or not. I'm living with you, aren't I?—Listen, you won't tell on me, will you? Then I'll tell you the secret. It's really great!'

'Bully for you.'

'You have to pretend you've got no idea when Mum tells you, okay? Like Christmas. I mean, when we're really really happy, even though we've sniffed everything out already. Because she told me I absolutely mustn't tell you. She wants to do it herself. So if you tell, I'll never give you my . . .'

'Yeah, okay. Spit it out.'

'You swear? By the holy mother of God and the sweet baby Jesus?'

'If you want.' I dampened two fingers, held them in the air, and she clapped her hands and smiled at me. She was wearing some brightly-coloured shorts and a vest, and when she pulled up her shoulders, they were narrower than her curly-haired head.

'Just imagine, Juli, we're going away! We're going on holiday! To Grandma in Schleswig!'

I put down my spoon of cornflakes, which was already almost in my mouth. 'What's that? When?'

She swung her feet back and forth so hard that they touched my knees. 'The day after tomorrow! The day after tomorrow!'

'You're crazy. Where've we got the money from all of a sudden?'

'No idea . . . We're going to the farm with the cows, and I'll get a pony and potato pancakes with apple sauce. And there are bikes too, Mum says. The sea's right behind the fields.'

'Then I could go fishing again! I bet Grandpa'll lend me a rod. And then we'll smoke the fishes in the oven and take them home. Last time I had two tenches and an eel.'

'I know. And you fell off a horse.'

'You can't remember that, you were much too small. Dad told you that. And I didn't really fall off, I sort of slid off sideways. You try riding without a saddle! It's not like on a merry-go-round; there's no bar to hold on to.'

'So what? I don't care. D'you think I can sleep in the hay?'

'Why not. Grandma's not so strict. Maybe we'll even find some eggs. Sometimes the chickens run off and hide them there.'

'Oh, great!' She lifted both her hands up in the air. 'I'm looking forward to it so much. I'm really in a good mood. Can't you sing me Maigret? Please Juli! Just a little bit.'

'Later. Let me eat first. How are we going? By train? Or is Grandpa Jupp taking us there?'

'Oh, I hope not! I don't want to go with Grandad Jupp. His car smells so disgusting, and he always puts his hand . . .' She started. We hadn't heard my mother's heels on the stairs, their tack-tack, or the key in the door; but the radio was suddenly on in the living room, and Sophie quickly took the tiger out of the milk and shook off the drops. She looked at me with wide eyes: 'You promised!' she hissed. 'Don't you dare give me away!'

We went into the living room. A wicker bag lay on the couch, and there was a small pile of swaddling clothes on the table. They were even freshly ironed. Holding Frau Gimbel's tiny baby, wrapped in a light yellow blanket, my mother was standing in front of the window, looking out onto the road and rocking to the song coming from the radio. She was humming quietly, and Sophie threw herself into an armchair. 'What's the matter? Is it sick?'

She turned her head, frowning, but didn't say a word.

'Well, it's not crying at all.' Sophie pulled up her feet under her bottom. 'Do we have to keep it for long?'

'She's sleeping.' Then my mother looked at me, at my dirty trousers, and I saw a brief flash of anger in her eyes. 'Have you had breakfast?'

'Yes, cornflakes. The stains aren't my fault. Fattie and the Marondes, I mean, there were three of them, and then I went flying into the ashes and . . .'

'It's all right, not so loud.' She looked at the baby and pulled the edge of the blanket up a little higher. 'That's what washing machines are for.' She pointed to the corner, at the flower stool; her cigarettes were next to the flower pot.

'Can you light one for me? Can you do that?'

'Who? Me? Sure . . .'

Sophie leapt up. 'Wait, I'll give you a light!'

My mother stared at her. 'Quietly, damn it!' She whispered. 'I'm glad she's finally gone to sleep.'

Sophie pushed out her lower lip and turned the wheel of the lighter; the flame shot up. I blew out the smoke without coughing, but when I handed my mother the cigarette she smiled vaguely, just with one corner of her mouth. 'Lighting the edge gives you crooked children. But never mind . . .'

She stroked the filter with her thumb before taking a drag, and my sister opened the bag, inspecting the little bottles and tins. 'Mum?' She smelled a honey-coloured dummy, touching it very carefully with her tongue. 'You wanted to tell Julian something, didn't you?'

'Oh really? Did I now?' With her head back, she blew the smoke up to the lamp. Then she blinked at me. 'What was it again . . . I think I forgot. Can you help me, Juli? Do you know what I wanted to tell you?'

I grinned, and she took another puff. Then the baby moved under the blanket, the tiny hands poked out over the edge, grasped at the air, and straight away it started crying, not very loudly. It sounded somehow distant and buzzing, the way our voices did through the telephones we used to make out of milk cans and string.

'There we are. Hold this!' My mother gave me the cigarette, laid the child on the table and unfolded the blanket. Sophie pulled a face.

'Did she shit herself?'

'Hey!' The buttons on the playsuit were made of clear plastic. 'What kind of way is that to speak?'

'What do you mean? Frau Gimbel says that too. Corinna shat herself.'

'But we don't say that!' She folded up the swaddling clothes into a little packet. 'Watch out that she doesn't fall down.' Then she went into the bathroom.

Sophie went to the table and bent over the baby. Its mouth was wide open, its eyes firmly shut, and it had a red head; my sister wrinkled up her nose, pushed her tongue behind her lower lip and mimicked the crying, though a bit more pitifully, holding her hands up to her temples like rabbit ears. I gave her a nudge.

My mother came back with a basin full of water and a washcloth. 'So Juli, listen.' She clasped both the baby's ankles with three fingers, lifted it up and washed its bottom. 'The way things are looking, I won't have an operation after all. But the doctor said I'm in urgent need of a break. Must be my nerves. So we could go to Grandma and maybe stay for two weeks. The only stupid thing is that Dad can't get any time off.' I sat down on the sofa and she looked at me, frowning. 'Why exactly are you still holding that cigarette?'

The standing ashtray was next to the armrest, and I put it on the dish. Then I felt the child's head, the fine black hair. 'But he could come for the weekend, couldn't he?'

It was sleeping again. She dried it off and pulled a big powder tin out of her bag, looking at the label. 'Oh Lord, Penaten. Just the same as you had.'

Sophie hopped about on the armchair. 'Riding, riding, riding! So are we going to the sea too?'

My mother shrugged her shoulders. 'Who knows, if the weather stays like this . . . But if I know your Grandma, she won't take a step outside her chicken farm. And if I'm there for once, she'll want me to stay around her. I can see it now: me running about through the rooms all day, carrying the coffee pot and cake tray.' She tried to open the tin, but didn't seem to be concentrating on what she was doing. While she looked thoughtfully out of the window, she turned the rubber lid—which wasn't even a screw top. It twisted, popped open, and Sophie covered her mouth with both hands.

The white powder, a thick cloud, covered the baby. One could hardly recognize the face anymore. But a moment later, after a single breath, the tiny nostrils were clear.

'Oh no! God almighty!' Our mother stared at us. 'I don't believe it. This can't be happening!' She spoke very quietly. 'What should I do?'

The baby kept still. It kicked its legs a bit and moved its lips; the powder mingled with saliva. The mixture ran out of the corner of its mouth, leaving a rosy trail across the white face. One could hardly see the hair anymore either, and the powder covered its eye sockets like flour on spoons. A few eyelashes poked out. Sophie went up to the table.

'Is she going to get black lung now?'

I stood up too, and my mother put away the tin and put her hand on her neck, slipping two fingers under her necklace. 'Julian! Say something! She's going to choke on me. What am I supposed to do? She's choking!' Her voice was suddenly hoarse, her lower lip trembled, and I took a step back. When she was helpless she looked much younger.

'So blow!' said Sophie, and my mother, nibbling at her thumb, closed her eyes for a moment and took a breath. The baby started coughing, little croaking sounds, and she reached for my shoulder, bent over the table and blew the powder off very gently. I could hardly hear her breathing. Slowly, as if under a layer of parchment that was being taken off piece by piece, Corinna's face appeared, and when I went over her mouth with my little finger to get the rest of the powder out, she opened her brown eyes and smiled at us, gurgling with joy.

'Good God!' My mother let out a sigh. 'The tins used to have screw tops . . . Sophie, get the vacuum cleaner, would you?' Her voice sounded normal again. She dipped a fresh cloth in the water and started washing the baby, and kept blowing up to her forehead as if there was hair hanging there. But she was wearing it up. 'For a moment there I didn't know . . . And to think I brought up two brats of my own. Oh, my nerves!'

She gave me a quick look and nibbled at her lower lip. 'Where were we? Oh yes, our trip. That endless bumpy train ride . . . But still, I think I could really use some recovery time. And I hope you'll help your father out a bit, won't you? I mean, Frau Gorny will cook for you two, that's been sorted out. But you could make his tea and his sandwiches, and go over the bathroom with a sponge now and again. Would you do that?'

There was a rattling in the kitchen, and the broom and scrubbing brush fell out of the cupboard. I still had powder on my hands, and rubbed it off on my chest. 'Who do you mean? Me?'

'What, am I talking to myself? Your sister told you, didn't she? I've added everything up. We can't stay with my parents, that tiny house is full. And the guesthouse is too expensive for three. I mean, your sister can come along for free, she'll sleep in my room. But you'd have to pay half the price, and we can't afford that with all the monthly rates for the TV, the couch and what have you. Do you understand me? You understand that, don't you?'

I nodded, lifted my shoulders, and she wrung out the cloth. 'Well then. You're a big boy, aren't you.' She laid out fresh swaddling clothes and smiled at the baby, pulling her lips all the way back from her teeth.

I turned round. The cigarette smoke rising from the ashtray was burning my eyes. Those Chesters really smelled of straw. I stretched out my arm and pushed the plunger, and the stub disappeared in the hammered metal container. The revolving dish made a sound like Sophie's old spinning top, except without the song.

The door to the hut was open, and old Pomrehn was sitting on the bench. He had slicked back his hair with water and was wearing a white shirt and suit trousers, but no shoes. The dog was lying on the floor in front of him, and he was stroking the back of its neck with one foot. 'Here comes our old warrior . . .' As if he had understood the words, Zorro turned his head and leapt up. I stayed where I was, and he panted and toddled about on the spot as if he didn't know what to do with himself. His left back paw kept giving way. Pomrehn grinned. 'He's happy to see you. He can tell the difference. Isn't that right, Zorro?'

The dog leapt up at me, pressed its paws against my stomach, and I stroked its neck, pulling at the coat like a pullover. It stank of dog food, and tried to lick across my face. But I lifted my chin and pushed it away. Then I bent down to pick up a charred stick, threw it into the bushes, and Zorro went running after it.

'Some hunting dog that is . . .' The old man shook his head. 'He's hunted himself. By his demon. Listen, I don't suppose you boys've got anything to drink stashed away here? A hip flask or something?'

I shrugged. 'Not that I know of. Haven't been here for a few days. What's a demon?'

He didn't look up, scratching the back of his hand. 'Nothing good, I don't think. Something you can't get rid of. Always follows you around.' Then he spat in the ashes, and Zorro came back with a rusty tin in his mouth and put it down in front of the hut. The brown spots on his greying coat gleamed in the sun, and he sat down between us, looking back and forth between the old man and me. Saliva was dripping from his tongue.

Pomrehn cleared his throat. 'This dog's a joke, isn't it? Look at the way he's listening to us. He doesn't even know he's a dog—he thinks he's a human. Non-smoker. But he used to get beaten, and he can't forget it.'

'Why do you think that? Because he's got such a funny walk?'

With his elbows on his knees, he folded his hands and stared in front of him. The white shirt must have been in the cupboard for a long time; the creases on the back had yellowed.

'Oh no, that's most likely a birth defect, something wrong with the hip. Here . . .' He stretched out his arm, made a fist, and Zorro stopped short and sank down into the grass. With his snout resting on his paws, he whimpered quietly and looked up to the old man, who frowned; it made him look severe, even grim. But as he suddenly pushed his fist forward, just for a moment, their shadows didn't even touch; but still the dog leapt up and took a step to the side. It stood there with its head below its shoulders and its neck hairs standing on end, legs slightly spread, and wrinkled its nose and flashed its teeth. It had pulled its tail in deep between its hind legs, and was growling in a strange way, as if there was something boiling in its throat, and got louder still. Saliva was dribbling from its lips, but Pomrehn didn't seem to be scared. He turned to me. 'You see? He's tasted a fist or two in his time.'

Then he opened his own, held out the flat of his hand, and nodded at the dog. 'Good boy! It's okay now.' His voice was suddenly deeper, and Zorro relaxed, sinking back into the grass. He wagged his tail, stirring up the ashes in front of the fireplace. Finally he crawled to the bench on his belly, smelled the old man's feet, and turned over onto his back, then let him stroke the fur on his chest.

I took a half-filled packet of Chester out of my pocket; it was already a bit squashed. 'How did you know that?'

Pomrehn, leaning down over the dog, looked up at me. He was smiling, somehow bitterly. His eyes were narrow, the folds in the corners like rays of light, and his nose had a bump on the top part, as if it had been broken some time. He closed his hand around the cigarettes. 'Well, I'm an old Indian, after all! Like you.'

All the Gorny children stood around the car, and Marusha also leaned over in front of the side window before going into the house. Her skirt was so short that one could see her knickers as she went up the stairs.

'Hey!' She stopped. With one hand on the banister, she bent her elbow and looked through her armpit. 'What are you looking at?'

I was carrying out my sister's travel bag and red suitcase. 'What do you mean? Nothing.'

'Like hell! You were peeking under my skirt!'

'Was not.'

'There! You're doing it again! I'll tell your mother about that, you little bastard! Then you'll be in for it!'

I twisted my mouth, my upper lip, so that she could see one of my fangs, and she bent over the railing and stuck her tongue out at me. Then she carried on up the stairs, and her bum brushed against the wallpaper as she moved aside to let my father past. He was carrying a suitcase too, the big brown one; the cardboard was grained like leather, just scratched up a bit at the edges. My mother was following him and didn't look up as she passed Marusha. She checked the contents of her handbag.

'Have a good trip, Frau Collien!'

'Thank you, I will. Look after my men, do you hear? And make sure you give them a hiding whenever they get cheeky.'

The girl gave a broad grin, winked at me, and I turned away. 'Where do the bags go? In the back?'

My father nodded, and when we went onto the street there were more children there. But Frau Streep and Herr Karwendel, who lived opposite us, were also standing there behind their fences, arms crossed, eyeing Grandpa Jupp's car. It was an American one, a Ford Mercury station wagon, black, with a cooler that looked like a predator's jaws. With their chrome edges, the tail fins also reminded me of a shark, and when the taillights and brake lights—which went across the whole width of the car—lit up, the asphalt changed colour. Little Schulz tried to see if he could scrape the white off the tyres with the tip of his shoe. He and his parents had only moved here recently, so he didn't know the car yet.

'Someone died at your house?'

I opened the tailgate and put the baggage next to the coffin. 'No. My mother and Sophie are going on holiday.'

'Oh.' He pointed to the lid full of white and salmon-coloured carnations. 'Is there a dead body under there?'

I looked at my father, but he didn't say anything. He pushed the suitcase over to the rest of the bags, and I shook my head. 'No, I don't think so.'

Little Schulz gave a sigh. 'Shame. Shall we play with the metal cars this afternoon? I've built a racing track.'

'Maybe . . . We'll see.'

I got in. The car only had front seats, a continuous bench of cream-coloured leather, and my father sat down at the wheel and turned on the ignition. I moved up next to him, and my mother, who had taken off her suit jacket, pushed the cigarette lighter and called Sophie through the open door. 'Are you coming?!'

She jumped over the Vogels' low hedge, came skipping around the car and plopped onto the seat so hard that a sweet fell out of her mouth. Anna and Rita, her friends, waved to her; they both had big gaps between their teeth, and she waved back at them as the car started. The engine hardly made a sound.

'Those stupid cows!' she whispered. 'They say we'll catch corpse rot and get a rash and everything. Is that true?'

My mother smiled. 'They're jealous . . . Watch out, Walter—the cat!'

My father steered the car onto Sterkrader Strasse. I looked at the speedometer, which wasn't round or oval like it was in other cars. It was a black rectangular screen on which a horizontal arrow appeared, which changed colour when the speed—measured in miles per hour—increased: white, yellow, orange, red, and later, when we drove on the highway for a while, even violet. In the cars we overtook, people's faces changed; they became strangely stiff. Here and there one could see vertical folds between their eyebrows, and their lips, which had been moving or had opened to laugh just a moment before, closed. And when Sophie clapped her hands, waved gleefully or pulled her faces, they gave each other blank, probably also dismayed looks, and it was only rarely that someone responded—with a quick nod or smile, as thin as air.

When we got to the station my father stopped behind the taxis, and a few people turned their heads when he took the luggage out of the coffin compartment. He looked at his watch, an old Kienzle with cracked glass. 'You've still got time. Go and have a sausage.' Then he handed my mother her jacket, holding it out with two fingers on the loop. 'Make sure Sophie doesn't swim out too far, you hear. And don't let her go to the mares in the paddock; they've all just had their foals.'

She nodded. She had a little golden unicorn with ruby-red eyes hanging on her jacket, and she folded the collar of her blouse over the lapel and plucked a hair off the sleeve. My father gave me a push.

'Come on, say goodbye. And then get in.'

I pointed to the luggage. 'Aren't we going to bring it to the train for them?'

My mother, whose nails were freshly varnished, put on a pair of white net gloves. 'Nonsense, it's not heavy. Look after yourselves. There's still some pasta salad in the fridge. And go through the house with a vacuum cleaner now and again.'

I wanted to take her hand, though that felt strange. But we had never hugged each other either. She smoothed out her skirt, the folds across her lap, while Sophie stood on tiptoe and looked into the glass drum of a raffle-ticket seller. My father got in and shut the driver's door. I was still standing.

My mother looked up. 'Well, what is it? Why aren't you getting in?' I didn't know what to say, and shrugged my shoulders. When I put my fists in my short pockets, the corners looked out from under the hem. I had old scratches on my knees. 'No street shoes indoors, you hear. Eat fruits, both of you. And don't forget the plants. Now hurry up, Juli, Dad's waiting.' She pointed to the car boot, where some of the flowers were already starting to wilt, and said quietly, almost in a whisper: 'You have to get the body to the morgue!'

I closed the tailgate and got in. The two of them waved, and my father pulled on the automatic gear lever. He backed up a bit, drove around an ambulance, and by the time we passed it again, my mother had already turned round and was talking to the raffle-ticket seller. But Sophie, holding her floppy teddy, came to the car again and knocked at the window.

'Juli!' My father braked. She put her mouth to the slit. 'I'll bring you some seashells, okay?'

We put our hands against the glass almost exactly at the same time, and then the car started again; I turned round and looked past the coffin into the boot. But the windows were frosted; the glass was only clear where two palm leaves crossed. Though even where they did, one could hardly see any more than the brick red of the station or the black of the taxis. And then my father was already turning the corner.

We drove in silence. Between us lay the overall he always wore when he helped Grandpa Jupp out. On top of it was a pair of rubber gloves, pink. It was hot; the air was shimmering above the asphalt. Two children in woollen swimming-trunks were balancing on the railing of the canal bridge, and jumped down with outstretched arms when they reached the middle. A dog barked aboard a coaler.

Grandpa Jupp lived in Sterkrade, opposite the Johanniter hospital, and he was already waiting in front of the door of his narrow shop. In the window, which had a pleated curtain, there was hardly space for more than a rubber tree and a single urn on a marble base.

Above the door there was gold lettering: *Hess. Under-takers*. As always, he was wearing a sailor's cap, and the cigar hanging from the corner of his mouth had almost burnt down. He looked at the clock. 'So, brought our darlings to the station, have we?'

My father reached under the dashboard and pulled the handbrake. Then he moved aside, and his stepfather squeezed himself behind the wheel. He wasn't very big, but had such an enormously fat belly that he had to sit far back, and could only hold the polished wood steering wheel at the bottom, with his fingertips. He pushed the stub into the ashtray and gave me his hand, the one with the blue signet ring. 'Hey there, son. Everything hunky-dory? Could do with a trip to the hairdresser, eh? Or are you already starting with one of those mushroom cuts?'

I grinned, and he started the engine and drove off, very slowly. He only touched the pedals with the tips of his toes, and he didn't look in the mirror when he changed lanes or turned off. But no one honked. When we got to Hagelkreuz he stopped at the traffic lights. 'So?' His voice always sounded as if he had a blocked-up nose. 'Are we going to take the lad home first?'

My father, his hands in his lap, must have nodded off. At least, he gave a twitch and looked up. 'Eh? No, that'll just take up more time. I'm on the night shift tonight.'

'On Saturday? My word. Finances looking any better?'

One of the display cases by the concert hall had been smashed, the other one had a poster for *Ursus the Avenger*. Grandpa Jupp looked at me from the corner of his eye. 'Ever seen a dead body?' I shook my head, and he turned off onto the graveyard behind the cinema. The gravel crunched under the tyres and shot up against the bottom of the car. 'Oh well, there's a first time for everything. They're only human, you know.'

We drove through an avenue of maple trees and stopped in front of the chapel. The front entrance was full of angels, and there were letters carved into the stucco that I didn't recognize. Grandpa Jupp noticed that I was looking at them. 'That's Greek. Alpha and omega. Do you know what that means?' I said I didn't, and he fingered a fresh cigar out of his leather case, then made a hole in the tip with a match. 'Neither do I. Probably makes of cars.'

We got out and went to the clinker brick building next to the chapel. It didn't have any windows, just skylights made of glass blocks, and we went past a row of numbered double doors, all closed. At the end of the corridor was a niche with a cross that had a bronze Jesus hanging on it, and my father reached up, pulled out a key from behind the INRI plaque and opened the last door, then pressed a switch.

A gust of cold, stale air blew into our faces, neon lights flashed on. An empty room, no bigger than our bathroom and with similar tiling; in the corner, next to a tub of periwinkle, two wooden trestles, and my father put them in the middle and made sure the legs were positioned exactly on the scratches that had already been made on the stone floor. Opa Jupp threw a black velvet blanket lined at the edges with brocade over them, and together we pulled and adjusted it until all four corners were touching the floor.

Then the men went out to get the coffin. The carnations on the lid wobbled as they carried it slowly along the corridor, and my father, who was walking backwards, looked at me over his shoulder. 'Prosper' was printed on the grey overall in faded letters.

'Hey, do *you* have our house key?'

I nodded, and they went around the corner and set down their burden on the trestles. With a cigar in his mouth, Grandpa Jupp was wheezing so hard that little flakes of ash flew off the glowing end. But he winked at me, bent his index finger and knocked on the varnished wood. 'Hello? Can we come in?' Then he undid the copper wing nuts and looked around; he seemed to be looking for a surface to put them on. Finally he gave them to me, and my father, who was doing the same on the other side of the coffin, handed me his. Carefully they lifted the lid and propped it up against the wall. A few carnations fell to the ground.

The deceased, an old, very delicate man under an ornamental quilt, had slid a little to the side, and Grandpa Jupp bent over him, pushed his hands under his shoulders, and straightened him again. Then he took a step towards the hallway, looked at his work, and gave an annoyed champ. He laid the cigar on the door handle, took hold of the body again, and pulled it a bit further up the pillow. Under its pearl-coloured cover I heard a crackling sound, as if there were wood wool or straw inside it. Now the head, with its sunken temples and handsomely arched forehead, looked out over the edge of the coffin, and one couldn't look up the nostrils anymore either.

The skin in the face was as white as wax, and his hands, which my father crossed on his chest—folding the fingers together—also seemed translucent, like watery milk. He was wearing two wedding rings, and Grandpa Jupp gave me a nudge.

'Now look at that! Over 80 years old, and he still hasn't had enough. Still wants to have a peek.' He pointed to the left eye, which had opened very slightly. One could see a little bit of the iris, grey, some yellow-ish white, and my father touched the eyelid with his little finger, closing it. As he pulled it back again, one could see the checked imprint of his gloves on the lid for a moment. But the eye opened again, maybe even a bit wider, the iris wasn't grey, but blue, and Grandpa Jupp shook his head. 'No no, Wally, it'll never work like that.'

He reached into his overall pocket and took out first a comb, then a pair of nail scissors, then a lipstick and a Lancôme powder tin; it was the same as my mother's. Besides that also a cotton pad and a tiny tube.

It almost vanished between his fat fingers, and while my father held the dead man's eye open, he filled out the lower lid with a liquid that smelled familiar. I stepped up to the coffin.

'What's that?'

Opa Jupp screwed the lid back on the tube. 'That? Don't ask me. Something for conjunctivitis, I think.' My father pushed the eyelids together and left his thumb there for a while, looking at his Kienzle.

The comb on the blanket had hairs of different colours hanging on it, and Grandpa Jupp went across the hall, opened a steel door and looked around. There was no one to be seen between the graves, and he bent down, plucked a few box-tree branches from an enclosure and spread them out on the blanket. 'Got to have a bit of parsley. You can put it all on the bill.'

The eye stayed shut, and we stepped back. The dead man looked content, even seemed to be grinning a little, and I crossed myself inconspicuously with my thumb. Behind me there was a snapping sound as my father pulled the gloves off his fingers.

Grandpa Jupp released the handbrake. 'Right, and now we've earned ourselves a nice roast.'

He drove out of the graveyard. The poster in the display case was being changed, *Hercules and the Wild Amazons*, and he took us to the centre of town, stopping in front of the bus stop. Then he ruffled my hair.

'We'll settle up next time, Wally. I'm a bit skint at the moment. Here's a fiver in case you want to send the lad to the hairdresser.' He gave my father a 20 mark note, and we got out and watched him drive off. Although he was headed in the direction of the Gute-hoffnungs-Hütte factory, he passed us again a moment later on the other side of the four-lane road. With his cigar between his fingers, he waved at us out of the open window.

The bus was almost empty. The only other passenger was an elderly woman. She had an imitation leather bag on her lap, and now and again I heard a mournful meowing coming out of it. Then she opened the zip and whispered something in a soothing voice. My father nodded off again. When the bus took a sharp turn by the swimming pool, he sank onto me and stayed like that for the rest of the ride. Though he was heavy, I didn't move. But I woke him up just before we got to the terminal.

There weren't many cars standing on the street, and they were all freshly washed. The women soaped them, the men wiped them down, and the children brought the water. When we got to our house, I rummaged in my trouser pocket and got a shock, then looked round. My father started.

'What's the matter? Lost the key? Come on, don't do this to me.'

'No, no. I thought . . .'

'So unlock the door!'

I took out the bunch. It had a rubber pendant, Carlo the Cat, and I ran up the stairs two steps at a time, and went straight into my room without taking off my shoes. Sophie's bed had been stripped, and my hand shook a little as I opened my chest of drawers and lifted up the clothes. I pushed my fist deep inside and closed my eyes involuntarily, as if that way I wouldn't hear the four wing nuts banging quietly against the wood.

The next day I arrived late at the sacristy. All the robes in my size were gone, and Herr Saale, the sexton, gave me an adult one and a rubber band. One had to tie it around one's stomach, and pull the part of the cassock that was too long over it. That made three layers of cloth, as well as the white cotton or lace robe on top, and I was already sweating before the High Mass began. The others were sitting on the long bench playing cards.

Reverend Stürwald looked at me. He limped; he had a real club-foot, with a special black shoe for it, and didn't mind giving the odd beating in scripture lessons. We called him Pastek. He pointed a finger at me.

'Can you read?' His robe was cream-coloured, and he was wearing a silver brocade sash, but his glasses were dirty; one could see fingerprints and dandruff on the lenses.

There was a sign hanging above the wardrobe: 'All altar boys must be in the sacristy at least 10 minutes before Mass'. The whispering and murmuring of the other boys stopped.

'Sorry, I overslept. My mother's away, and the alarm clock . . .'

He waved his hand dismissively. 'I'm not interested.' Then he opened a leather-bound book, one of the big ones, and held it out to me. His thumb was yellow. 'Read this passage here. Nice and loudly.'

A text in Gothic lettering. The illuminated first letter was printed so boldly that I could feel the motifs, the leaf garlands and little birds, under my fingers. 'The fathers ate sour grapes, but the children's teeth were blunted when they tried. For behold, all men belong to me; the fathers belong to me just as the sons do; all who sin must die.'

'Very nice.' Stürwald coughed; his breath smelled of smoke. 'Sounds good. You can be lector. Make sure you don't turn two pages at once; the gold borders stick together. And now come on, get in position!'

He handed me the lavish book, and I stepped to the head of the procession and looked around. Only the older altar boys got to be lectors, and often the job was done by adults; but that Sunday everyone was younger than me. I knew that little Schulz, who was standing right behind me, didn't even know the Confiteor by heart, just mumbled when it came around, and I breathed deeply as the sexton rang the little bell, then lifted the book up to my chest. The door was only open a crack, but I could see that the church was full.

But in my excitement I forgot to adjust the rubber band quickly one last time, to pull it up under the gown. Like most of the ones in the drawer it was worn out, and it had slipped down from the top of my stomach to my hips, along with the whole mass of cloth it had to support. The organ was booming, the congregation was singing, and as I couldn't change anything with the heavy book in my hands, it didn't take long for me to step on the hem, which pulled it down a little further.

Even though all the doors and skylights had been opened, it was breathtakingly hot. There were even people standing in the aisle, and I had to kick the red cloth along in front of me with each step just to make it all the way to the altar without stumbling, which made a wild flapping and fluttering sound. A few adults in the front row grinned. A little girl covered her mouth with her hand.

Herr Gorny was there too. He was standing between the men and the women, and looked at me unblinkingly for a long time. He squeezed his eyes together, and his thin lips twitched, before he turned the page in his hymnbook with a dampened finger. For a tiny moment I saw the fingertip through the thin paper, and probably got even slower. Stürwald cleared his throat. Little Schulz pushed his folded hands against my back.

My father cycled to the mine along the dusty path between the fields. He was wearing his brown corduroy jacket with the leather collar, and soon he was no more than a speck in the distance, then disappeared completely into the copse in front of the winding tower. The sun was low. The cat's eye on his mudguard twinkled one last time.

The shadow of the weather house, with its pointed gables, spread across the whole wall of the balcony. I was sitting in the corner under the empty swallow's nest eating yoghurt when I heard the door in Marusha's room creak. The curtain blew over our table for a moment out of the open window, and then I heard music, the Beatles, and leaned forward.

She was wearing the chequered skirt and a bra, and the red sky flared up in the big mirror as she opened the laundry cupboard. She had to stand on tiptoe to get to the top shelf, which made her calf muscles stand out. Some paper fell on the floor, two squashed handkerchiefs, and she opened the bra, hung it on the door handle, and pulled a white shirt over her head; it was pretty tight. I could see her nose and chin under the fabric as she pulled at it, as well as her open mouth, and she stamped on the floor impatiently.

I had never seen my mother's breasts, but even when she was wearing her bodice they weren't as full as Marusha's, which bobbed up and down a little. There were very fine blue veins that disappeared at the sides, and the nipples hardly stood out from the brown skin, which almost looked golden in the evening light. But there was a hair gleaming on one of them.

The record finished, shot out of the player, and she stretched out her foot and pushed it back in again. Then she discovered me through the crack in the curtains, and seemed to freeze. For two or three heartbeats she cast a threatening look in my direction from the mirror. Then she carefully pulled the material down from her chest to her navel, turned round, and swiped at me through the curtains.

'Hey, you peeping tom! Piss off!'

I shrunk back, but stayed in my seat.

'So, what are you waiting for?! You should be ashamed of yourself . . .'

'Why? This is our balcony. I was eating yoghurt here.'

She tore the drapes aside and glared at me.

'Yoghurt, my arse! You were gawking at my tits!'

'Was not. At your back.'

'So you *were* looking in here!' She lifted her hand, and I pushed myself further back into the corner. The granules in the roughcast wall pricked my arm.

'If you're going to leave the window open! Where am I supposed to look. I live here, you know . . . You want a fag?'

She lifted her chin and pulled on her earring. But her angry expression became a little softer. 'Horny bastard!' She smiled strictly. 'Your old man home?'

I shook my head. 'He's just gone. Doing the night shift. But his Gold-Dollar is lying over there, on the couch.'

'Nah, don't worry. They're too strong for me.' She sat on the windowsill, pulled up her knees and turned round on her bottom. Then put her feet on our table. Her skirt had slid high enough for me to see the white triangle between her thighs, the ugly fold in the material. I looked over the railing to the garden, where Herr Gorny was sawing branches off a fruit tree. Marusha pushed out her lower lip and blew a strand from her forehead. 'Phew . . . this heat really wears you out, doesn't it? Have you been swimming?'

'No. It's too far for me.'

'Far? What do you mean? You've got a bike.'

'Not me, it's my father's. I can only take it when he doesn't have to work.' I spooned the rest out of my glass and licked the spoon. 'So what's happening with your job? Are you working at Lantermann?'

'Where? Oh, you must be joking. I'm at Kaiser und Gantz!' She wrapped her arms around her shins and rested her head on one knee. 'Trial period. But you needn't think I'll stay there. They just push you around. Working in the storeroom, the cloth bales heavy as rocks—can you imagine what that's like? And as soon as I'm finished and about to go to the front, where there's air conditioning, that stupid cow points to my blouse and says: "You can't show yourself to the customers with those sweat patches, young lady." So I go back to the storeroom and have to put up with them groping me as well. Thank you very much!'

'So do something else.'

'Oh yeah? Like what? Scrubbing floors at Hoesch? Or should I go to the chocolate factory and wear an overall and bonnet?' As she moved her feet, her toes left delicate imprints on the tabletop, but they dried instantly. ' "Grow yourself a belly," Jonny always says, "then you'll get welfare." That's what he's like.'

'But why? You don't have to eat the chocolate. Just wrap it up.'

She frowned for a moment and shook her head. Then she smiled. 'You really are sweet . . . has your mother written yet?'

'No. They've only just left.'

'And you two are lonely, eh? But now you've got the house to yourself. Why don't you invite your girlfriend!'

'What? Why are you always going on about that stuff! I don't have a girlfriend. I'm only 12.'

'You're almost 13. Old enough to get up to plenty of mischief. I got drunk the first time when I was 12. So who d'you like in your class? Do I know her?'

'It's only boys in my class.'

'But in the parallel class? Is there someone there?'

I shrugged, wiping out the yoghurt bottle. 'Don't know. Maybe.'

'So who is it? Come on, spit it out!'

With a finger in my mouth, I mumbled the name.

But she still managed to understand it, and opened her eyes theatrically wide.

'Angelika Dezelak? The one with the queer brother? Harkordstrasse? You can't be serious!'

'So what? Why not?'

'But she wears thick specs, doesn't she? And she's almost a head taller than you. What d'you like about that beanpole?'

I stood up. 'None of your business. We're exactly the same height. And she's funny. But everyone teases her because she's always scared. They call her four-eyes, things like that.'

'And that's why you like her?'

I didn't answer, went to the kitchen and rinsed out the glass. But Marusha leapt up from the table and followed me.

'Come on, tell me! You're in love with her just because the others take the piss?'

'Rubbish! We go to school together sometimes, that's all. Or we play cards, like animal quartet. What're you doing here anyway? This is our kitchen!'

But she pushed me aside with her hip, turned on

the tap and put her mouth to it. The water ran down her chin and onto the shirt. Then she put her hands underneath and then behind her head. 'Have you two kissed yet?'

I didn't say anything, just gave a snort, and she opened our fridge, looking at the different shelves. Apart from margarine and condensed milk, the only things in there were a bottle of beer and a bit of brawn. She took the little bottle of nail varnish out of the butter compartment and compared the colour to her own nails. 'Kissing's important. Most boys can't do it. Kissing and being affectionate. They always want to . . . Even if a total dog comes along; just ask Jonny. He doesn't care if a girl's ugly or has bad breath or whatever. You know what he says? He'll just put a towel over her head.'

I sat down on the dresser; now I was half a head taller than her. 'Why a towel? Then he can't see her.'

Staring at the garden through the window, to the rows of young fruit trees in front of the shed, Marusha curled a lock of hair around her index finger. A few drops of water, as clear as dew, were glittering on the branches where they had been sawn off. Herr Gorny slit open the bark with a box cutter and carefully removed it partly from the wood. He did that twice with each stump, then wrapped a few small branches cut off at a very steep angle in an old swaddling cloth in the grass. He dunked them in a pot of glue and pushed them behind the bark.

'So have you ever kissed anyone?'

In the light shining on her legs from the fridge, I could see Marusha's goose pimples in the cool air, and I gulped and shook my head, but didn't manage to say a word. Although she hadn't moved, she suddenly seemed very close; I could smell her breath, more chewing gum than smoke. 'Then it's about time you learnt, isn't it?'

She gave me a quick look from the corner of her eye, pushed her tongue into her cheek, and her bare feet made a quiet sound on the floorboards as she turned round and went to the front door. It had been left ajar. 'How long's your father working the night shift?'

'What? No idea. A week.'

She stepped onto the mat. 'Interesting. And you're all alone? Then I'll come and pay you a visit, sunshine.'

I grinned. 'No way! Everything gets locked up here.'

She pulled her chin back onto her neck and grunted mockingly. 'As if that'd stop me . . .' Then she disappeared into her room, and I slid down from the dresser and closed the fridge. Down below, Herr Gorny was tying up the stumps with bast.

'By the way, they're looking for someone to help out at the co-op.' But she was already out of earshot.

I took the broom out of the cupboard and filled a bucket with water. After I had added a shot of washing-up liquid I looked for a cloth, but all I found was an old shirt that was hanging on the bend in the tubing under the sink. It was full of holes, and I put everything in the hall and swept the stairs. Someone was playing the accordion in the Gornys' apartment, probably Lotte. She was the youngest, and could hardly look over the top of the instrument. Usually Frau Gorny sat next to her and helped her open and close the bellows while she practised a scale.

I swept the dust out of the doorway and into the garden, then wiped the steps one by one with the wet cloth. The sun was shining in through the skylight, and the reddish brown wood shone as if it were freshly varnished. Then Wolfgang came into the hall. The stirrup between the braces of his leather shorts had an edelweiss made of horn stuck on it, and he bit off a piece of sausage and chewed it loudly.

'Hey! Why are you making the stairs wet?'

I didn't answer, and wrung out the cloth. But he stayed there. The mean look in his eyes had something to do with his parting; but I couldn't say what.

'That's some hunting dog you've got at the club! I've never seen a beast like that. It's sick, isn't it? Keeps doing somersaults and slobbering everywhere. I'd have it put to sleep.'

I carried on wiping and didn't look up. 'You're just angry because you weren't made a member. Four votes against one—and that was yours.'

'Oh, rubbish. That's kids' stuff anyway.' He spat something out; a tiny piece of gristle fell to the floor and bounced across the tiles. 'I'm going to high school now.'

'Well great, Seppel. That's where you belong.'

He seemed to say something in reply, but I couldn't make it out. With loud cries, Dietrich and

Sabine, two of his younger siblings, raced past him into the open, and he followed them and closed the door. I wiped the last step and threw the cloth into the bucket. Lotte took her fingers for a walk across the piano keys, and I walked up the slightly winding staircase to go back home, whistling as I went. But after a few steps I saw that I was leaving footprints on the damp polish. So I went back down and started moving up the stairs backwards, wiping away my tracks.

That took longer than the actual cleaning. I was sweating and almost at the top when the front door opened a crack. Whispering and giggling, Dietrich and Sabine looked up at me with liquorice traces in the corners of their mouths. Their faces were hot, and for a moment I saw a pair of braces behind them, the horn edelweiss. Then they raised their thin little arms and threw two handfuls of garden soil across the steps, almost at the same time. Small stones flew all the way up to me and were still bouncing down the stairs when the door had already fallen shut again.

'Stamp collectors!' No idea why I shouted that. I couldn't think of anything else in my anger. The sand crunched under my shoes, and on the step before last I

RALF ROTHMANN

slipped, but just managed to catch myself. I stormed out, but there was no one on the pavement. All I saw was Wolfgang's bike on the stand, the groove in the paving-stone, and I spat on the saddle. Then I went through the corridor and knocked on the door of the ground floor. The accordion fell silent.

Frau Gorny, whose bandaged legs meant that she could only shuffle along, opened up. She was chewing something, and smiled down at me over her tremendous bosom. 'Well? Still hungry?' She had made us a big pot of barley soup, enough for the whole week, and I shook my head and pointed at the steps. I was still slightly out of breath. Lotte was standing behind her, looking at me with her mouth open, and her mother frowned and took a step into the hall. 'Well, what is it?'

I swallowed down my saliva. 'I cleaned up, and then . . . the mess over there . . . Wolfgang did that. He told Didi and Sabine to do it, and they came with some dirt and . . .' I made a movement with my arm, looked up at her, but she made a face as if she didn't understand. Rummaging in the pockets of her apron, she shuffled back indoors. Her bandages smelled of tar.

'Why are *you* cleaning the stairs?'

I shrugged. 'They were dirty.'

'Yes, but it wasn't our dirt, was it? You're the ones who go up there. We live down here.'

'Sure. I know. But the sand and the stones . . .'

She shook her head and put a dried apple ring in her mouth. 'No, no.' There was fluff from the apron sticking to it, but that didn't seem to bother her. She champed quietly. 'My children don't do things like that. They've been brought up properly.' Then she closed the door.

The man pushed the wagon through the mined-out space. It went slightly downhill, and ended in an unsecured stable shaft. In a pile of old gin traps there was a warning sign, and behind a diagonal wooden cross there was a drop of 20 metres. The shift was over, and one could barely hear anything except the wailing of the air blown through the ventilation shaft. The dust swirled through the beam of his lamp, and the man locked the wheels, put on gloves and cleared away the irons, which were linked together in several places. Then he set up an additional light, unfolded his yardstick, and measured the height of the coal face.

The wood in the mine car was new and smelled of resin, and he sawed off half a dozen beams and wedged them in between the lintel and the threshold. The hammer strokes echoed through the shaft and the adjacent shaft botto.ns as he nailed one board after another to the squared timber pieces; the narrower the opening, the louder the blowing of the draught became, and it finally became so strong that it blew his scarf over his mouth. Then the shaft was braced, and he put away the rest of the wood and the tools, put out his lantern and pulled the wagon back.

Although the rails were rusted, the wheels rolled almost silently, and once he had reached the end of the slope, he stopped at a drift crossing with what they called a 'scythe extension' to tighten his shoelaces. Then he took his dented tin bottle out of the wood pile, shook it next to his ear, and drank what was left in it. He loved that hour after the end of the shift, when most of the miners had long since gone to the coop or were sitting on their bikes, that rich uneventfulness in which one didn't have to do or look at anything all the time. In which one felt sensed by the mountain. It was cold.

There was a distant smell of limestone.

He wiped his mouth with the back of his hand, snapped the lid shut, and put the bottle in his jacket. The semicircular steel beams arched over him like the ribs of a giant ribcage, and he took a deep breath and pulled the car along—then something seemed to be moving high up, silently and weightlessly. As if one darkness were inserting itself into another. As if the air were twitching. There couldn't be bats anymore here, almost a thousand metres below ground, and he looked up and turned round. The spot of light, trembling, floated over the marl and steel. Marl and steel.

Somewhere a coal cutting machine wailed and fell silent again. Chains rattled, and he went on. The smell of limestone became stronger, and then he could hear it—the familiar shuffling of the dusters, the clatter of their buckets and their rhythmic shouts. Four head-lamps approached, surrounded by a greyish-white cloud, and the man stepped into a niche, an abandoned drift, and pulled his scarf over his mouth and nose. 'Duuust!' called out the foreman, who was wearing a red helmet and waving to him; 'Duuust!' repeated the others in unison and reached into the buckets that hung on their

shoulders. With great force, each of them threw a handful of lime onto the level and the stopes at the sides of
the drift to bind the coal dust and eliminate the risk of
explosions.

They went past him in small, synchronized steps,
and their arm movements too were as perfectly co-ordi-
nated as those of sowers. Those at the front covered the
lower part of the drift, and those who followed took
care of the crest. They had tucked their jacket sleeves
into their gloves and their trouser legs into their socks,
but none of them was wearing a filter; the masks were
hanging from their belts. The fifth man, who was following at a certain distance and seeing to any spots that
had been overlooked, was holding a cigarette in his
cupped hand, and as the line turned the next corner,
everything that had been black was white.

The sheet of paper in the newsreader's hands trembled,
and she didn't look up. She had already misread the
phrase 'Warsaw Pact states' three times, which I found
so embarrassing that I felt like hiding behind the armchair. I turned off the sound and went to the kitchen to

make myself a sandwich. The moon was covered by clouds, and the street lamps in Fernewaldstrasse seemed to be flickering; but it was probably the masses of moths that were creating that impression. The wheat fields rustled, and sometimes I heard a distant rumbling. Maybe there'll finally be a storm, I thought to myself. No light in Marusha's window.

I peeled the skin off the sausage—and then the doorbell rang. A short, muffled sound, as if someone had knocked against the button by accident. I would hardly have heard it in the bathroom, and I ran through the living room and looked out onto the road, but all I could see was a cat rubbing the back of its neck against the edge of a switchbox. The bicycle mirror screwed onto the windowsill by the previous tenants to keep an eye on the entrance had been turned away.

The bell rang again, just as briefly and probably just as quietly; but I could feel my pulse in my throat. The buzzer was in the hallway, and as I stepped onto the doormat I got such a shock that I almost screamed, and took a gasping breath. Marusha put her hand over my mouth. In the bluish flickering of the television I could see that she was wearing shorts and a sleeveless blouse;

she also smelled of perfume, and I reached for the switch.

'Have you just come home? Why didn't you turn the light on?'

But she held my fingers tight and hissed at me; her breath smelled of toothpaste. And suddenly someone dashed up the stairs—on the inside, where the wood didn't creak. With his pointed shoes in his hand, he went up two steps at a time, and his shadow grew above him and his glistening quiff, then got smaller again. There was a bottle sticking out of the back pocket of his trousers.

Without a word, he disappeared through the door Marusha was holding open for him, and although she shut it again straight away, I had seen the candle, an Avon aromatic candle like the ones my mother had. She stroked my cheek with the back of her hand.

'You won't tell on me, will you? Jonny's got some time off. We just want to talk about something.'

She had whispered, and I also spoke quietly. 'It's okay, don't worry. Are you going to snog him?'

'Don't be cheeky, sunshine. Go and sleep!'

Then she pushed me indoors, shut our door from the outside, and I turned the key and went to get my sandwich. On the television, still without sound, there were miners with blackened faces squatting in a low drift extension and waving to the camera, and for a moment I listened. But all I heard was the quiet crunching of my jaws.

In a Jerry Cotton book I once read how a murderer got into a locked apartment by pushing a piece of newspaper under the door. He poked about in the keyhole until the key fell onto the paper, then pulled it out to one side. And then he unlocked the door . . . I stuffed the rest of the sandwich into my mouth, then took out the house key and put it in my pocket. After that I poured myself a glass of milk.

One could see the moon again; the clouds were clearing above the winding tower, and I carefully lifted the lever and pushed open the door to the balcony. Far away, in the valley behind the fields, I heard the rumbling of the freight train that connected the mines and coking plants; occasionally something banged against the rails, and I tried in vain to make someone out behind Marusha's curtains. The coarse fabric was too thick; one couldn't even see the candlelight through it. But one half of the window was tilted, and I carefully sat down on the chair underneath it, which wobbled a little. The long train got quieter from time to time, then rattled along twice as loudly under the bridges. I counted four of them. Then it turned off behind the waste dumps, and it was so quiet again that I could hear a hedgehog at the end of the garden, its snorting and groaning as it squeezed under a fence post with its spines. For a second I saw the moonlight sparkle in its tiny eyes.

Marusha whispered. She seemed to be shaking up the bedclothes, and Jonny answered in a very muted, deep voice; I couldn't understand a word. There was a snap, probably from the lid of his bottle, and right after that I heard a quiet, almost silent gargling. Marusha gave a very short laugh; something metallic rattled, maybe a buckle. Her whispering got louder and more breathless at the same time, the bedsprings squeaked, and then it was quiet for a while; I thought they had fallen asleep. The smell of lavender from the candle wafted through the window crack, and I drank up my milk and put the glass on the railing. Not a sound in the garden either. The hedgehog was gone. The leaves on the trees glistened.

A warm breeze stroked my face, the leftover drops of milk ran down the inside of the glass, and suddenly Marusha cried out; it was a muted cry, as if she had her face in a pillow, and something crashed about in the room. I shot up, but stayed where I was. The silence that followed had a feeling of expectancy, and I tried to hear whether anyone was stirring in the house; her stepfather was a light sleeper . . . But everything stayed silent. The only sound was the dripping of the tap above the sink, and then Marusha groaned again, more quietly than before.

But it sounded pained, like a cat having the scruff of its neck twisted, and I cleared my throat, took the glass to the kitchen and rinsed it out. It slipped out of my hand, but didn't break. Then I opened the fridge, stared inside, couldn't remember what I wanted, and shut it again. When I stepped out onto the balcony again she was still groaning. I also heard a sound that was familiar, a sort of clapping, which reminded me of my mother. She didn't beat my sister as often as me, and not with the wooden spoon, as Sophie was still little. But she hit her with the flat of her hand, usually on her naked bottom, and that was exactly what it sounded like behind the curtains, just not as loud.

I thought about what a brute Jonny was, and that he always found some reason to get in a fight, every time the fair was on. He seemed to have wet hands, and I imagined Marusha's face, covered in tears, and him slapping it again and again while she tried desperately to defend herself. The old bed, which my father had once repaired for her with wire, was creaking and groaning, the rounded gable with the fruits carved into it knocked against the wall, and I cleared my throat again, this time exaggeratedly. But they didn't seem to hear it.

Because suddenly, as if she had given him a kick in the stomach, Jonny groaned loudly and seemed to sink into the pillows. It sounded like a growl through bared teeth, like Ursus lifting up rocks or enemies—while Marusha breathed very quickly and shakily and then laughed quietly. A golden wheezing. Then there was silence.

A few moments later I heard a match being lit. Smoke came through the window crack, the aroma of a Roth-Händle, and I went to the living room and turned off the TV, which only had the test card on the screen. Sat down on the couch again. I went through the spaces between my toes with my fingertip, but there was no dirt there. The lantern in front of the house projected the shadows of the pot plants under the ceiling, and the greyish-black jungle of overlapping leaves and branches in front of the delicate pattern on the curtain seemed to move. But it was the water that was welling up in my eyes—no idea why—and I curled up and fell asleep.

Some time later I heard a quiet creaking, footsteps going down the stairs, and I felt cold; but I felt too sluggish to get up, and covered myself with the brocade cushion. In my dream I was banging against a coffin lid again and again, calling my name, and suddenly I sat up with a start. Morning had come, and I spent a moment in surprise that I was wearing my clothes. Then the knocking got louder, an angry hammering; the door rattled on its hinges.

'Julian!'

I recognized the voice and pushed the handle. 'It's locked!' I called out, and he banged against the wood again.

'I can see that! Open the bloody door!'

It was only now that I remembered the key in my trouser pocket, and when my father came into the room I took a step backwards, away from his vacant gaze. He was pale, almost white, as he always was after a night shift.

'What's wrong with you? Why did you lock yourself in?' He looked around, and I yawned, maybe a little exaggeratedly, and rubbed my face.

'What time is it? Shall I make you a Nescafé?'

He didn't say anything, still waiting for an answer. The edges of his eyelids were still black from the coal dust.

'Well, I wasn't going to lock the door. But then there was a scary film, someone with a knife got into a house, and I thought . . .'

He snorted mockingly and put his bag on the glass cabinet. 'Are you crazy or something? A film's a film, and you're you. Who's going to do anything to you here?'

I shrugged and straightened the cushions. 'Nobody.'

'Well then! Leave that damn TV off, will you!' Then he buttoned up his shirt and went into the bathroom.

Zorro whimpered as I poured a bottling jar full of barley into his bowl. He pulled a piece of sausage out of the mash with his pointed teeth and ran into the garden. The rabbit cage was empty, and the pigeons weren't in their enclosure either. Only the cockatiel was left, dozing motionlessly on its perch under the ceiling. Its grey eyelids were shut, and it didn't even open them when I poured some grain into its bowl, just moved along a bit.

I swept the hut and took the tin bucket to the pump behind Pomrehn's house. One had to push down the handle a few times before the first water, which was still rusty, came out. If it came at all. The old man's kitchen window was open, so was the glass veranda, which consisted of lots of little panes, many of them cracked. The window putty had crumbled away almost everywhere, and whenever the door fell shut the whole porch rattled. But now the morning sun was shining through it, and a pale red blossom had opened on one of the cactuses on the shelf.

The door inside was ajar, and behind it there was a laundry room with a big tank they used to cook pig feed in; there was still a sour smell coming from the walls. There was no one in the garden rooms, and I went through the corridor full of chests and cupboards that led to the other part of the house. The sunflowers in front of the living room window were the head-high, and light only came into the room at a few points here and there, in dusty sunbeams that kept being broken up by the shadows of the birds. I knocked on the door-frame.

Pomrehn, who was sitting among his machines, didn't turn round. With his hands in his lap, he was staring at the floor in front of him. His white hair was flattened against the back of his head. 'Julian! What have you brought me?'

'How did you know it was me . . . ? Just wanted to see how you were.'

'Oh, good.' He pointed to a carton of cigarettes that had been torn open and a bottle of Doornkaat on the shelf. 'I think I'm a welfare case now. They've impounded the house, taken it away right from under my arse. But never mind. As long as they let me die here.'

'What do you mean? Are you sick?'

'I wish.' He lit a Reval. The smoke spread sluggishly through the room. 'My wife says I have to keep going. I'm not finished yet.'

'Your wife?'

He nodded. 'And I always ask her: "Why, damn it? What haven't I finished?" But she doesn't tell me, of course.'

I grinned. 'She can't, can she. She's dead. Do you have any idea where the rabbits are? The hutch is open, and no one . . .'

'What do you mean, dead? That's all rubbish. Just because someone goes down into the grave, doesn't mean they're dead. Maybe they go away for a while, like in a dream. But then they come back and don't remember anything, you understand?'

I shook my head and sat down on a stool. He was standing in front of the machine with the round brushes, some of them made from animal hair; they felt like pony manes. 'My grandpa makes money with dead people. I mean, he's got one of those undertaker's shops. And it's not nice for you at all if you're lying there dead. They almost break your fingers, and then they smear glue in your eyes so they stay shut.'

Pomrehn unscrewed the Doornkaat and took a gulp. 'Oh no. That's not death.' He wiped his mouth. 'That's just dying . . . you want to know where the bunnies are? Ask your mates. Or you might as well just go and have a look in their oven.'

'What?' I got up. 'You mean they slaughtered them? The little white one too?'

'Nah, that one wasn't so small anymore. And it was me that slaughtered them. Those kids were much too daft, messing about with their blunt knives. Instead of grabbing them by the ears and then taking a poker and smack, breaking their necks . . . they wanted to skin them while they were still twitching about.'

I reached into a box full of heels, took one out and turned it about between my fingers. 'But the white one was mine! It was called Mister Sweet.'

Pomrehn smacked his lips. 'Well . . . what can I do, my boy. They said they'd arranged it with you.'

I threw the heel hard back into the box. 'Those liars!' It sprang up again, and I ran out, took the half-filled bucket from the pump and brought it to the hut.

I looked around for Zorro under the fruit trees and tried to whistle. But my lips were tense with anger, and my mouth was so dry that I couldn't make a sound. After giving the cockatiel some water, filling its little feeding bowl, I took my spear off the wall. The tip, the flattened-out nail, had broken off, and I pulled the rest

of it out of the wood and carved the words 'You fat bastard, you're going to die!' into the door. Then I left.

The wheat fields behind the Kleekamp estate were
already being cut. Clouds of dust rose to the sky, which
was full of swallows, a plane with a banner was doing its
rounds, and I made my way through the gorse bushes
until I got to the edge of the gravel pit. My shadow fell
across the yellow slope, and I shielded my eyes with one
hand and looked at the bottom of the pit, where the
dry soil was broken up like a honeycomb. Nobody was
playing down there; it was probably too hot, and I lifted
my head. A light, but very loud machine—'Persil always
stays Persil'. In front of the door hung a chain, the pilot
was wearing shorts, and when I looked at my shadow
again there was a dog squatting next to it a distance
away. But I didn't turn round, not even when it started
whimpering quietly.

There was a rusted sign at the edge of the pit:
'Danger of Collapse'. It sloped down steeply for a bit,
and I broke the spear over my knee and threw one half
down to the bottom. Zorro started, growled, and
stretched out his neck. Then I flung the second half,
and he dug in the grass, turned around himself once
and then—leapt in after it. The tail, which was full of

thistles, was almost flat, his ears flew up and for a moment his shadow darted ahead of him.

But as soon as he touched the ground his legs failed him, and he howled and rolled down the slope, almost invisible from all the dust. The clicking of the stones and pebbles sounded like bones to me, and sometimes he writhed about as if he were a sack of sand, without a spine. It was only slightly before a silo that had over-turned and was lying on the ground that he managed to get to his feet again. He sneezed, shook himself and looked up at me. He looked so small down there, yellowish-grey, and I tapped my forehead.

'What *are* you doing, you stupid dirtball! D'you want to break your ribs?!'

He barked, then cowered in fear of his own echo. The reverberations from all sides got him so worried that he sank down onto his bottom, the pointed shoul-der blades higher than his head, and I jumped down, landing softly on the loose soil. But getting to him wasn't so easy; with every step I sank in up to my an-kles, and the pebbles in my shoes hurt, and when I finally got to the silo, Zorro hadn't moved an inch. With his front paws spread and his long tongue hanging out of the side of his mouth, he looked at me, panting. One ear was folded back, and I straightened it out in passing, which stirred up some dust.

Then I marched across the pit towards the entrance, a gravel ramp, and while he ran across the slopes, dug in holes or lapped up muddy water from bike trails, I looked at the junk that was lying around everywhere: dented ovens, mattresses, rubble. I had a box of matches with me, and every now and again I lit one and threw it into one of the paint buckets or rusted canisters. But nothing exploded.

When we came out of the pit I walked along the bike path for a while, peering into the gardens. All the Gorny children were out in the yard. They were sitting on homemade benches and shining shoes. Everyone had their job: Dietrich brushed off the worst of the dirt, Sabine put brown cream on, Lotte black cream, and Wolfgang polished them. Frau Gorny was standing at the kitchen window peeling potatoes.

I turned round and ran across the road with Zorro. Just before we got to the hedge I tried to knock the dirt off his fur, and he bit into my shoelaces; he wanted to play, and was already rolling about in the grass again.

So I gave up, clicked my fingers and ran up the steps to the front door. He followed me with a leap.

But when I opened the door, he seemed to freeze. He pushed his paws against the doorway, sniffed at the floor tiles, and I grabbed him by the collar and dragged him up the stairs, walking backwards. Saliva dribbled out of his mouth, and he rolled his eyes and scratched at the wood with his claws; but I didn't stop, just kept going up, almost pulling the leather over his ears. His tormented growling echoed through the hallway, he snapped at me, and when I stopped on the landing to catch my breath he broke free with a sudden twist of the head.

But luckily he didn't run down again. He jumped past me up the stairs, and as the door was locked, he couldn't get any further. With his tail between his legs, he turned around on the spot and looked into the upper corner of the pointed space as if the little spider there could help him. Then he sank down onto his mat, whimpered quietly, and slowly I went up to meet him.

'Good boy! No one's going to hurt you!' I showed him the palms of my hands, smiling, but his eyes were full of fear, and when I reached the top he jumped back onto his paws. His whole body was shaking, and his urine was splashing onto the floorboards; I was going to shout at him, but kept calm. I reached carefully over his head for the handle, and as soon as I pushed it down he squeezed through the crack and darted blindly until he got to my room. Crawled under Sophie's bed. I followed him and closed the door.

My father was still asleep, and after I had wiped up the piss I drank a cup of water. Then I put the crank on the bread slicer and cut a few slices of the bread Frau Gorny had put out for us. I spread margarine and liver sausage on them, then put the immersion coil in the kettle for his tea. We had Penny Royal and Westminster; I took Westminster. There was still half a lemon in the egg compartment of the fridge, and as I squeezed it I heard him in the bathroom, then a bit later in the living room.

My mother's glass cabinet rattled gently whenever he walked across the floorboards. It was an old cabinet with a semicircular base that barely came up to the hips of adults. Behind the faceted glass door there were three shelves; on the two lower ones were her ornamental cups, which stood on top of their saucers in such a way that one could look inside them, at the flowers or gold ornaments, and the compartment above that held our glasses for wine and liqueur, almost all wafer-thin. But we never used them, not even on Sundays. My father drank his beer from the bottle, and our milk came in old mustard glasses with handles. On the cabinet stood the smoke eater, a porcelain owl; its eyes glowed yellow when one turned it on.

My father yawned. He was still wearing his pyjama trousers and a vest, and scratched his stomach and chest with both hands. Then he put the pot with the barley in it on the small hotplate borrowed from Frau Schulz, and I snapped the lunchbox shut.

'I put liver sausage on it is that okay? If you'd prefer cheese I'd have to go shopping quickly.'

He shook his head, pulled the teabag from the thermos flask, and put in a tablespoon of sugar and the lemon juice. Then he screwed on the lid, and once the barley was warm he took a plateful and sat down on the balcony. But he didn't eat. His hands in his lap, he was staring across the fields and the woods in front of the mine with a dazed look on his face. There were flocks of crows circling the winding tower, and he scratched a bit of scab off his arm, an old scratch. The skin underneath was rosy.

With the dishcloth over my shoulder, I sat down next to him. He closed his eyes for a moment, gulped, and I pushed the bottle of Maggi sauce across the table to him.

'Have you spoken to Mum?'

'Hm?' The whites of his eyes were completely clear again, and he didn't look so pale anymore either. He stirred the barley. Then he ate a spoonful, and I could just make out a slight frown. 'I called her. But she wasn't in the guesthouse.'

'Where then? At the stud farm?'

He chewed slowly, somehow carefully, and shook his head. 'Went to the sea, the landlady said. Have you done your homework?'

'Maths? Did it yesterday.'

While he seasoned his soup, I opened the drawer under the table; my sister kept her plasticine in there. Marbles rolled towards me, and I shut it again. Then I pointed at the window behind me with my thumb.

'Hey Dad, I wanted to ask you something. That's really our room, isn't it?'

He broke some bread onto his plate. 'What do you

175

mean? It belongs to our apartment, yes.'

'So why can't we use it then?'

'Ha, you're a fine one. And where's the Gorny girl supposed to go?'

I swatted a fly on the railing with the dishcloth. But it was already dead. 'Don't know. Maybe she'll get married soon or just move out. Would I get the room then?'

He took a swig of milk from the bottle and wiped his mouth with his thumb. 'Could be. If we can pay for it.'

'What? I thought it was part of our flat!'

'Course it is, smart arse. But we pay less rent for not using it.'

'Oh, right . . .' I moistened my finger and rubbed some dirt off my knee. My father was chewing on something gristly; I heard it cracking quietly inside his mouth. But instead of spitting it out he kept chewing, and his teeth made the same grinding sound they did when he was asleep. I looked into the garden.

'So, Herr Gorny's a miner too, isn't he?'

'Of course. Everyone here's a miner, you know that.'

'But he's not the same kind as you, is he? You're his superior, aren't you?'

'Sometimes. If he gets assigned to me. He's a hewer, and I'm a shaft supervisor.'

'So then you can tell him what to do?'

He shrugged, then nodded.

'And you earn more money too, don't you?'

'A bit. If the contracts are made properly.'

'But then why does he have a house and we don't?'

'Oh, so that's what you're getting at.' He pushed the half-full plate away and ate another piece of bread. 'Well, he has a house, but then he'll also be in debt for the rest of his life. It's his bank that owns it, not him. And I'd never choose that. I want to be free, you understand? You as an old Indian . . .'

I grinned. 'Tecumseh! He who moves with the wind.'

'Well, there you go. And I'm like that too.'

The vest stretched across his chest, hairs stuck out through the fabric here and there. I stood up and got his cigarettes out of the kitchen. 'But you have to work, don't you?'

He hesitated, then sat up. 'What was that?'

I had heard something too, and gave him his lighter. 'Don't worry, you stay there. I'll have a look. Maybe a book fell off the shelf.'

In our room, Zorro had knocked over my sister's box of dolls and was just tearing up one of her teddy bears. Wood wool spilled out of its stomach, one ear was only hanging by a corner, and when I tried to pull it out from between his teeth he growled threateningly, so I let him keep it. But put the box on the cupboard.

'It was just a doll falling off the bed.'

With a cigarette in his mouth, my father was standing in the living room getting dressed, and I packed the sandwiches and the tea into his bag. He buttoned up his shirt. 'Maybe we'll win the lottery. A house'd be nice, sure. Somewhere green. No one else, a bit more space . . .' Then he wrinkled up his nose. 'Hey, did you step in some dog muck?'

I held onto the cupboard and looked at my soles. 'No. Maybe the smell's coming in from outside. Shall I get you the bike from the cellar?'

He said no, took his jacket off the hook and gave it a quick shake. The keys rattled. 'Don't go to bed so late, you hear? There's nothing but crap on TV anyway. And once you've got it in your head, you'll never get it out again. What was that letter in the bin, the scraps from Spar?'

'A what? Oh, an ad.'

'How do you know? It hadn't been opened, had it?'

'The Gornys had the same one.'

He nodded, went out, and a few moments later I saw him between the yellowish-grey fields, where he quickly got smaller. The sun set, and the chrome bicycle clips on his trouser legs flashed every time he pedalled. I got myself a clean spoon and ate the leftovers from his plate, and it occurred to me that none of us played the lottery. Ever.

The following night, Marusha wedged a piece of cardboard between the bell and the beater, and when it buzzed I didn't answer the door. Or rather, I only went to lock it. It seemed Jonny hadn't taken off his shoes and was carrying a bag, maybe a plastic bag, full of bottles, and I stepped out onto the balcony and leaned against the railing. The window was open, but the crack between the curtains was too narrow to see anything. And the bedside lamp was also shining on the rust-coloured cloth.

The cupboard door squeaked, and suddenly the music, a song by the Rolling Stones, was turned up loud. And then turned down again straight away. Jonny gave a fake dirty laugh, seemed to be opening a beer; the bedsprings creaked, and a moment later he burped, making a dark bubbling sound. 'Hello from level seven . . .' Marusha giggled, turned off the lamp, and now the red curtain was grey; I saw my narrow silhouette, projected onto the cloth by the moonlight, and withdrew.

Zorro was sleeping on the sofa with the TV on. But when I sat down next to him he woke up, and I scratched his neck, plucking a few thistle spores from his coat. 'You really do smell, mate. Like an askari.' I had no idea what that was; my father said it sometimes when he was telling us about work: 'We stank like askaris'. Zorro bit my hand playfully.

I went to the kitchen, unwrapped a piece of sausage, and held it high above my head. His tail banged against the glass cabinet. He followed me to the bathroom, whimpering, and after I had closed the door behind him I let my hand down and threw the morsel into the bathtub. He hesitated, lifted his paws up to the edge, but couldn't reach high enough, and I grabbed him by the hind legs and helped him in. His claws clicked against the enamel, and he gobbled up the sausage and barked once, as if to thank me. Licked his lips.

I stroked his head, pushed my fingers behind his collar and turned on the tap. Though it was still hot from the afternoon, he shuddered when the water came spraying out at him from the shower head. He wanted to jump aside, his paws squeaked and creaked on the tub, but I held him tight and spoke calming words. His wet coat now looked black.

He growled and rolled his bloodshot eyes, and while I poured egg shampoo down his spine, a long stream, he reared up. But I twisted his plaited leather collar so that he could hardly breathe, not even howl or bark, just gasp. The tension in my arm was like in the autumn, in a storm, when one holds onto a distant kite by a string. But I still held him tight, even when he started slipping in the foam and kept banging against the edge of the bathtub, the fittings. And finally he seemed to give up.

He stood there with his legs apart, shaking, and I soaped him thoroughly and rinsed him off, twice. The water was grey, but his coat, which clung tightly to his bony frame, felt softer again, and I draped the white bath towel over his body and rubbed him down. He put up with it. When he was partly dry, I reached under his ribcage and helped him out of the bath, where his claws had left a few scratch marks, and opened the door. But he didn't look at me, and didn't follow me in front of the TV. He trotted off to my room and crawled back under Sophie's bed.

I lay down on the couch. There was a love story on the second channel, and when the couple started kissing, I kneeled down in front of the screen to see exactly how they were doing it. Their lips were closed, not a trace of any tongue movement, and I found it strange that they didn't collide with their noses, which were long. It must have been because of the way their heads were tilted, and I took a soft pencil and drew a face on the doorframe—dot, dot, comma, dash. Made the lips a bit clearer. Then I put my hands on either side of the wood, around hip height, and pushed my lower body forwards. If I moved straight towards the face, the tip of my nose soon hit the frame. But if I tilted my head, my nose went over the edge and I could kiss the mouth without any obstacles.

I practised that a few times, with my eyes shut as well—when there was suddenly a knock, just a very quiet one. Someone pushed the handle down, then did it a few more times, but I didn't react. What I did do was spit on my fingers and wipe the drawing off the painted doorframe, which didn't quite work; I just smudged it. There was another knock, a bit louder this time, and I looked at the alarm clock. It was 11.

'Who's there?'

'Well, who do you think,' Marusha hissed. 'I hope you're going to open up soon!'

'Why? I'm already sleeping.'

'With the telly on?! Please . . . ! It's urgent.'

I pulled on the string and switched on the standard lamp. Then I reached into my trouser pocket, put the key in the lock, but only opened the door a crack. I kept my foot in front of it. Marusha was wearing her dressing gown with the Disney pictures. It was from Woolworth's, and whoever made it hadn't paid attention to the pattern at the seams. A piece of Goofy was joined to one of Minnie, and Uncle Scrooge's hat was on Pluto's bottom.

'Can we use your toilet? We were talking and drank a bit too much beer . . . my washbasin's broken.'

'And why don't you use your potty?'

'It's full!' She rubbed her knees together the same way Sophie did when she could hardly take it anymore. 'Please, Juli! I'll give you something too.'

'All right.' I stepped back. 'But not dark chocolate again!'

Jonny, whose quiff was as straight as if he hadn't been in bed at all, put a hand on her shoulder and pushed past us. His black swimming trunks shimmered like coal and had a stain at the front. He hardly looked at me, just went straight into the hall through the living room, and had already disappeared inside the bathroom before I managed to say 'Right!'

Marusha smiled at me. 'He knows that.' It was a serious smile, a woman's smile.

'Oh yeah? How?'

She shrugged her shoulders. 'The houses are all the same, aren't they.'

He hadn't closed the door, and we heard his pee splashing into the toilet, but she didn't seem embarrassed. She looked around the room.

'You've really got nice furniture, I must say. Your mother's got taste. One day, when I've got a place of my own . . .'

'Why? Are you moving out?'

'Me? You'd like that, wouldn't you? Well, who knows . . .'

Her dressing gown wasn't done up very tightly, and I thought she smelled funny, like Rotkäppchen Camembert. I pointed to her neck. No idea why, but I suddenly whispered: 'Did he choke you?'

She opened her mouth, which looked as if her lipstick had been smudged. But she wasn't wearing any. Next to the front door was a round mirror with a star-shaped frame made of wool threads and wire, and she touched the two reddish violet patches on her neck and mumbled: 'The dirty bastard!'

At that moment Jonny pulled the chain, the water gurgled in the plumbing, and as he walked towards us he was still fiddling with the string on his swimming trunks. He didn't even try to walk quietly. His chest was hairless, the muscles there twitched with every step, and he grinned at us. But Marusha's eyes flashed with rage.

'What's this here, you arse! You got a screw loose?'

'Why?' He winked at me. 'A little mark. So everyone can see you're Jonny's.'

'Oh really. And how am I supposed to explain that at work? You can imagine what they'll think! I can't serve people with a scarf in this heat!'

He clicked his tongue quietly and made a movement with his head. 'Stop yacking. Go and piss.'

She took a deep breath, but didn't say anything. She tightened her belt with a jolt. Then she turned away, and her bottom wobbled under the coloured cloth; her brown thighs glistened. Jonny looked at me.

'It's her own fault, that's all I can say. If they're so horny they don't even notice . . . right? How old are you, shorty?' He smelled of hair mousse and beer.

'Me? Almost 13.'

'Twelve then. Got hair on your balls yet?'

I didn't answer, just gave a little snort, and he laughed. 'Don't get upset. You're not a girl, are you.

Want to go for a spin on my Guzzi?'

'Excuse me, don't you have a Kreidler?'

'Don't be so formal. I *had* a Kreidler. Why?'

'Is a Guzzi better?'

'Better?! That's like Goggo and Mercedes, man!'

Lots of homemade tattoos on his arms—anchors, burning hearts, a cross on the hill. And some writing: 'Jonny loves . . .' I turned my head slightly, but couldn't make out a name. There was a gap after 'loves', a pale oval. Then the next image, a water-nymph with a sword. The toilet flushed again, and Marusha came out of the bathroom without looking at us. With her fists in the pockets of her dressing gown, she squeezed her lips together into a thin line and looked at the TV as if there were more to see than the test card.

Jonny stretched out his arm. 'Don't make a fuss. Tomorrow the spot'll be yesterday's news.'

I suppose he wanted to smack her on the bottom, but she dodged and ran her hand over my hair. 'Thanks, Juli. And go to bed, you hear. It's late now. I'm going to sleep too.' With her chin up, she left the apartment without even a sideways glance at the man. But he winked at me, and a few moments later I heard her giggling again in the dark. A song by the Beatles finished quietly.

I took a slice of sausage out of the fridge and threw it under Sophie's bed. Zorro sniffed at it and smacked his lips, but didn't come out. That is, until I dangled a second piece under his nose. He was still a bit clammy, but didn't seem to be angry with me anymore. His coat smelled good. I put a dish out on the balcony for him, poured milk into it, and his tongue lapped about in it so excitedly that the porcelain rattled on the stone floor. But even though their window was tilted, the others didn't seem to hear it.

The bed creaked, the springs groaned, and Marusha breathed quickly and shakily, then sighed quietly. I didn't hear anything from him, and I sat down on the floor, leaned my back against the wall, and looked at the sky. The dog also lifted its head once. There was something silvery to the sounds, very delicate, like moonlight on milk. I felt the hairs on my forearms standing on end, and scratched across them.

An aeroplane flickered between the stars. They were moving harder now, Zorro licked a few drops off the stones, and I held my breath when Marusha suddenly whispered 'Wait a minute! Wait!' Immediately there was silence, I heard house crickets chirping in the garden, and then something rustled, probably pillows, and her voice behind the curtains sounded normal again, very quiet, almost grown-up. The dish was empty. 'Julian? Can you please go back inside?'

I stood up, pulled the dog through the doorway and closed the door.

The man turned round. The lights up to the bend in the head drift worked, albeit flickeringly. Water had broken in at three points, but the way to the shaft seemed to be clear. Behind that it was dark. That was the beginning of the Old Man, a mined-out coal face that hadn't been filled up yet and was used as an escape and a storage space. The entrance was flooded, and he opened the box next to the scraper, took out a mallet, a saw and a handful of nails and went to the sheet piles a miner had stacked there before being surprised by the water inrush. They were a good two metres long, and he sawed one of them in two, connecting the halves with crossbeams. Next to the stack there were several canisters of water and tea, and he emptied two of them into the darkness—which suddenly seemed to become a memory lighter. Peppermint.

Then he pulled out a reel of wire from between the tools and fastened the plastic containers under the boards. He pushed the raft into the water, put his tool-box on top, and laid the demolition hammer next to it. A winch screeched somewhere, and he took off his jacket and grey vest and undid the buckles on his shoes. He stuffed his socks inside, pulled the belt out of its loops, hung it across his upper body and fastened the battery for his headlamp to the front of his chest. Finally he stepped out of his heavy canvas trousers, put everything on the raft and took a few steps down the sloping level.

Despite the heat in the drift, the water wasn't warm, and it kept getting colder, almost icy, the deeper he probed. The sudden reflections of his lamplight dazzled him, and he felt the rails under his naked feet and held on to the props, shaved roundwoods that protruded from the water like remains of prehistoric pile buildings. It came up to his knees, and with the next step his navel disappeared.

He stood still for a moment so that his body could adjust to the temperature, which at least had something reliable about it under the circumstances. He looked up slowly. Almost everything up there, the hanging wall, was now only supported by the rock's internal stress, and every drop that fell out of the cracks and crevices echoed several times in the silence. A row of trapezoid support beams was leaning against the drift wall at an angle, looking like a burnt-out roof truss.

He waded on, now up to his chest in water, but his lamp didn't flicker; the battery was watertight. Under his feet there was rubble and pieces of iron, and when he stopped feeling the ground for a moment he held onto an old air line, crumbling rubber, and pulled himself along by it. A few moments later the level rose again, and he looked around. A mess of supports and struts that had fallen over or collapsed lay behind him, and between them there were chains and cables hanging down like vines; they were submerged in the smooth blackness and surfaced again further along. But there was something lightly-coloured floating very close to him, and he shone his lamp on it. A lunchbox, plastic. It was slightly transparent in the light, and he could make out something in gold wrapping inside it, maybe a sweet, a chocolate, and took a step towards it.

He paddled with one arm, and the raft, which he was pulling along behind him, drifted to the side and brushed against a prop, which stayed where it was. But the cap on it, a raw spruce trunk, splashed into the water, which still came up to his ribs and surged up above him. He took a step forwards, but wasn't fast enough. The tree trunk, carried up again by the force of its impact, scraped across his back. He bared his teeth and squeezed his eyes together tightly.

He forced himself to breathe deeply, even though he was hardly able to for pain. He only wheezed, his stomach muscles drew themselves together, and he began to feel giddy. He held on to the raft with one hand, and with the other he touched his back and then looked at his fingers in the lamplight. Then he sank deeper into the water; as dirty as it was, its coolness did him good. A gauge door opened somewhere, the draught became stronger, putting ripples in the black surface, and he looked around for the lunchbox again. But a tangle of scalloped props, that had fallen on top of each other in all directions, blocked his view, and he straightened up and walked slowly on.

The bird was gone. Someone had got in during the night and smashed everything to pieces, probably a few of the Kleekamp gang. They had taken anything they could use—returnable bottles, candle stumps, tools—and even shat in the corner. Green flies shimmered on the pile and flew up when Zorro went to smell it. With my knife I cut out a piece of the cardboard that covered the floor and threw the muck into the cornfield. I hung the cockatiel's perch on a tree.

They had also torn up one of the nudist magazines from the secret compartment behind the wall panel; there were shreds of naked girls lying everywhere, and I swept them out over the doorway. Then I looked for a stone the right size and nailed the boards up again. The little window had only been left hanging by one hinge; the other one couldn't be screwed on anymore, as the holes were worn out. But I put in some wood, tiny shavings, until I could get a hold on the screw again.

As I shut the window—the church bells were ringing, though I was sure it wasn't noon yet—I saw him between the walls and the charred beams of the old stable. He was stroking Zorro's head, and seemed to be reading the inscriptions and markings on the plasterwork; maybe he had heard me. Or maybe not. I pulled

193

the flimsy rag in front of the cracked glass, which already had moss growing in its corners, went to the door and very carefully pushed it shut. It still creaked.

But he didn't turn round. He rummaged about in his tattered bag, which had a thermos flask sticking out of the top, put something in his mouth and carried on reading as he chewed. Fattie and the others had written all sorts of dirty stuff on the walls, rhymes too—'A hole's a hole, it's the place for your pole'—and on the metre-long willie of a garden dwarf, a drawing by Karl, stood our names. I pushed the little bolt shut a bit too early, and had to pull the door open again, just a crack. But just then Herr Gorny turned round, and although the trees stood between us, it felt as if he were up close, looking straight into my eyes. He didn't seem surprised. He tipped his hat.

'Hello.'

I just nodded, and he gave Zorro a bit of bread, closed the bag and came slowly through the grass. He eyed everything that was lying around: an old ladder, a wheelbarrow without a wheel, piles of broken tiles, and I stepped under the canopy. There was a crumb stuck to his chin.

'Well?' He pushed his hat up from his forehead and looked past me at the hut. His eyelashes were blonde too. 'So that's your hideout? Not bad. And where are the animals?'

I shrugged and pointed at Zorro. 'At the moment we've only got him. A pedigree hunting dog. Obeys my every word.'

Herr Gorny came closer, and I stepped aside. But he still laid a hand on my shoulder; I wobbled a little. He stepped through the doorway and looked around and curled up his nose. The brown material of his suit gleamed on his sleeves and the backs of his thighs, and he put his bag down and pointed to the corner with his thumb.

'And what's that? A kid's coffin?'

I grinned. 'That was the feed box. But it's empty.'

'Well then . . .' He sat down on the lid and laid both hands on his knees, where one could hardly see the trouser crease anymore. His wide wedding ring flashed in the gloom. 'We used to have huts like this too. If our parents had known what kind of things we got up to in there . . .' He held out a palm and folded his fingers into it quickly several times. 'Come in for a moment and close the door. So I can see what it feels like in here.'

'But I have to hold on to the handle. Otherwise the door'll open again. Have you already finished work?'

Zorro was scratching about in front of the door-way, and Herr Gorny clicked his tongue and pointed into the room. 'You could make something out of this. A table here, a bed there, a little stove—and there's your love nest. A right house owner, aren't you? Like me.'

'No. It doesn't belong to me.'

'Hey, I was only joking. But my house doesn't be-long to me either. Not really.'

'What do you mean? Who owns it then? The bank?'

He looked at me out of the corner of his eye, a quick glance, and pushed one hand into his trouser pocket. 'Not them either. You can't own anything in life, you understand?'

I frowned.

'Yes you do, you understand. You go to church, right? Not a hair on your head belongs to you. Not one.'

. ▮

'You mean because they could fall out?'

'Or you might keep them. But that doesn't mean they belong to you. Think about it, think hard about it. And then try saying: my money, my house, my wife . . . it's all not so important. Underneath my clothes I'm just like you.' He looked around again. 'So this is where you play your little games?'

'Sometimes. Car quartet. Or Mau Mau.'

'Come on, you can't fool me. You do other things too.'

'Really? Like what?' I didn't know what he meant, and he bent over and lifted up a stamp-sized bit of paper. He smirked, but his mouth was as thin as a razor's edge.

'And what's this?'

Flesh-coloured. I had overlooked it when I swept the hut, and shrugged my shoulders. 'No idea. Maybe it belongs to the Kleekamp gang.'

'Don't give me that. You think I'm stupid? You lot wank here, don't you?'

'What?'

'My God, you don't have to be embarrassed. It's normal, we did it too. So who's got the biggest one?'

'What do you mean? I don't know. I just feed the animals.'

He snorted mockingly. 'Yeah, right . . .' While he rummaged in his trouser pocket with one hand—the shape of his knuckles pushed through the thin material—he held the little picture in front of him with the other. His thumbnail was a bluish-black colour.

'I should be going now, because my father . . .'

'He's on the night shift. He's sleeping. Relax, son. We know each other, don't we? We live under the same roof. Have you been getting a flickering on the TV screen too lately?'

'Us? Not really. Only on the test card.'

'Oh really? Interesting.' He rummaged harder in his pocket, which seemed to be costing him quite an effort. He closed his eyes, then groaned quietly. 'So you watch TV so late . . .'

Zorro's paws appeared under the door, just the tips; he scratched at the cardboard on the floor, and Herr Gorny leaned back.

'Your father's a well-built man. Muscular . . . the women like that. Have you ever seen him naked?'

'Me? No.'

He licked his lower lip. 'But I have. We all see each other the way we were born. In the coop. We wash each other's backs, you know. There's nothing wrong with that. There are big ones and little ones. Bent ones and straight ones. Some are even circumcized. Would you like to see?'

The dog was howling outside, and I didn't know what to say. I felt my arm, the fleabites on my elbow, a whole string of them, and now Herr Gorny was rummaging about in the other pocket; it made a metallic sound, like pastilles in a tin. He breathed in sharply through his teeth and pulled his knees far apart. I opened the door.

'Hey, wait a minute!'

'Yeah, just a moment . . .'

But I went outside after all, squinting in the sunlight. 'Are you looking for your house key? You can have mine. I still have to clear up here anyway.'

Zorro greeted me with a bark and leapt up at me. He pressed his paws against my chest and tried to lick my face, but I pushed him away. I had to pee, went under the trees, and he followed me, toddling through the stream. A few moments later Herr Gorny came out of the hut.

I was just taking the rabbit hutch apart; it smelled pretty strongly, and there was still some fur stuck to the rough boards. He had put his hat back on and was fiddling with his zip. As he did so he smiled at me, and for the first time I saw his teeth. They were yellow and short, and stood slightly apart from one another. I broke a piece of wood over my knee.

'My word!' He brushed dust and cobwebs off his sleeve. 'Strong, aren't you.'

I didn't want to grin, and broke the next board in half. But then I did grin after all, and he pulled the door shut behind him. I stacked the wood in the furrow.

'Come on . . . a boy your age doesn't squat down anymore when he's doing something on the ground. That's what squirts and little girls do. Stand up and bend over!'

'Yes. Did you find your key?'

He just shook his head and stepped onto the asphalt bike path, where I saw a smashed reflector lying on the ground. After looking at it for a while, he kicked it away and turned round again. A sudden wind stirred up the wheat behind him, two sparrows flew up from it, and he grabbed the brim of his hat. 'Tell me, do you get bored when your father's on the night shift? Do you feel alone?'

No idea why I suddenly felt a stinging in my eyes. The wind blew cold ash up in the air, and I shook my head. Then I stacked the rest of the boards and a few rotten branches on the pile and looked for my matches. 'I don't watch TV till late at all. The test card also comes before the programmes start.'

He gave me a look that wasn't exactly unfriendly; but although he had blue eyes, his gaze was somehow grey. 'I see. Maybe I'll come and visit you some time, shall I? I often can't sleep either. Then we can play cards or something. Car quartet.'

I didn't say anything, just nodded, and he went away. I had got the matchbox wet once, and lots of the sulphur heads crumbled against the striking surface. I finally managed to light some paper, but the wood didn't burn well, probably because of the wind. It blew clouds across the sky, stirred up the fallen leaves and pushed the flame to one side. Wilted grass caught fire, and I stepped on them. But the flames kept spreading, I trampled and trampled, and my shoes sent clouds of dust flying up from the dry soil.

On Sunday we had a late breakfast, without ornamental cups. My father made us scrambled eggs with some chives that Frau Gorny had brought up from the garden, and we ate with the TV on, a breakfast show—*Der internationale Frühschoppen*. I didn't just find Werner Höfer unpleasant because of his glasses. He always spoke in such a drawn-out way, so that one already knew what he would say next and got the feeling this boring programme would never end. But then my father turned it off and lit a Gold-Dollar. He laid both arms on the backrest of the sofa and looked out of the window. The sky was blue.

'Have you called Mum?'

He nodded. 'Last night, before my shift.'

'So? Are they coming back next week?'

He leaned his head back and blew the smoke upwards. 'More like the week after. Your mother needs a bit of a break.'

'Sure.' I pushed the ashtray over to him. 'Maybe we could visit them some time? For a day or so?'

He looked at me. 'That'd be nice. But I'm on the night shift again next week—Bored, aren't you?'

'No, no. It's all right.'

'Yes you are, you're bored. You'd rather be up there too, like me. We're both real country bumpkins, eh?'

I grinned and shrugged my shoulders. Then I stood up and put the plates together, took them into the kitchen and poured myself another glass of milk. A flag had been hoisted on top of the mine's winding tower, because of Berlin.

'Listen . . .' He took a sip of his Nescafé. 'We can go on an outing. I've got a mate at Kleekamp, and I've always wanted to pay him a visit. A decent bloke. We'll go there.'

'Well . . .' I sat back down. 'We don't have to. I'm really not bored.'

He put out the cigarette and pulled the belt of his dressing gown tighter. 'You'll like him. Knows all the players in the Western second division, every score. And he collects those military magazines and photos of battleships and stuff like that. And guess what: his brother's a real criminal. Do you remember that diamond robbery two years ago in Amsterdam?' He pointed to the Sunday paper lying in the fruit bowl. 'They got away with tens of millions. And Lippek's brother was one of them!'

'Is Lippek a nickname?'

'What? No, no. That's his last name. He's called Herbert—All right then, I'll go and shave now, you wash the dishes and clear up a bit, and then we'll be off.'

There was a strange smell when I went into the kitchen again, familiar and off-putting at the same time, and I looked out to the balcony through the open door. Marusha was sitting on the window sill, varnishing her nails. She had her feet on our table, and didn't look up.

'Hey! Are you in a bad mood?'

The little brush flashed in the sun. She didn't say anything, just shook her head slowly, and I turned on the gas boiler and let some warm water into the sink, then added a shot of washing-up liquid. I took another look from the corner of my eye. She was wearing her Lee jeans and a sports shirt, and I rinsed out the ashtray and washed the dishes, but couldn't get the frying pan properly clean. There was a bit of egg stuck to the pan, and Marusha screwed on the lid of her bottle.

'You won't get anywhere with that cloth. You need

a steel sponge.'

I had no idea where to find anything like that in the kitchen. I looked under the sink, and she plucked the cotton wool out from between her toes.

'In the broom cupboard. On the top shelf.'

There did turn out to be a steel sponge in there, and Marusha stretched and yawned. Then she stuck out her legs so far that her feet went over the edge of the table, and looked at the fresh red on her toes. 'These Sundays are the pits, aren't they? You look forward all week to a day off, and then you don't know what to do with it. I think I'll emigrate. To Holland maybe, where those drop-outs are. They don't have to do anything, but still live well.'

'You could go for an outing with Jonny. Rowing in Grafenmühle. And they have shooting ranges there too.'

'Who?' She curled up her nose. 'He can keep away from me, that wanker. Don't you turn out like those guys, you hear! I've had just about enough of it.' She held out a fist and winked at me. 'Can I trust you with that?'

I went out onto the balcony. The patches on her neck had grown paler. But there were new ones on her forearm, blue bruises, and I took the cotton wool out of her hand.

'By the way, we're going out in a minute. To a real diamond robber. He was even in the papers.'

'Where? How's that?'

I threw the flakes into the coal scuttle. 'My father knows him, from the mine. Him and the others took millions, a while ago in Amsterdam. Didn't you read about it?'

She smirked. 'Oh yeah? And because he's so rich he goes to the mine everyday, or what?'

I shrugged. 'No idea. He was there, anyway. Him or his brother. You can come and ask him if you want.'

'You think so?'

'Why not?' I carried on scrubbing away at the pan, without much success; the brown coating got the sponge all stuck up, and my father came into the kitchen. He was already wearing his suit trousers, and was buttoning up his white shirt. He normally had trouble with the top button because of his big hands, and now too he bent forwards a little, stuck out his chin. I wiped my hands on my trousers, and while I did up the button he looked into the sink. 'That's the sponge for the toilet, son. For the lime scale . . .'

He didn't seem to have noticed Marusha. With his arms around his knees he bent over. Her voice was bright and friendly, as it always was when she spoke to my parents, and she gave a wide smile. But only with her mouth.

'Hello, Herr Collien!'

My father gave a quick nod and cleared away the clean dishes. The top shelves of the wall cupboard were still too high for me. She took her feet off our table and put them on her windowsill.

'Juli said you're going on an outing?'

'Rubbish. We're going for a walk.'

'You're lucky. Can't I come too?'

'You? What for?'

'It's so boring here.'

He pushed his collar up and took the tie out of his bag. 'Then go and help your mother. There's always something to do, you know.'

'It's my day off today!' She pouted sulkily. 'I need a break too.'

He looked in the mirror above the sink, a leftover

from the cage of the budgie we used to have, and tied his tie; his fingers were trembling slightly, the way they usually did when he had to do delicate things. 'You're not even dressed properly yet. And we're going now. Maybe next time.'

He put the end of the tie through the loop, and she sat up. There was a yellow emblem sewn to her sports shirt, the German eagle.

'I only need one minute. Thirty seconds. Please, Herr Collien! Juli said I could come.'

My father looked at me from the corner of his eye. I scratched away at the pan with a wooden spoon, and he shook his head. 'All right, why not. But we're only going to Kleekamp. Tell your parents.'

She bit her lower lip, smiling. Then she lifted her feet, turned round to her room, and a moment later we heard banging and rattling, as we always did when she rummaged about in her wardrobe. I folded the dish-cloth together, hung it over the oven handle, and my father gave me a clap.

'You're an early starter, aren't you . . . comb your hair, you hear. And then take off those shorts, please.'

I went into my room. But the khaki trousers were

dirty, and I put on the ones from my communion suit and rubbed the crease. But it still stood out. Then I got a comb from the bathroom, and while I was still trying to get it through my hair, there was a knock at the door and Marusha stood in the living room, beaming at us.

'Can I go like this?'

My father, who was sitting on the sofa and leafing through the newspaper, hardly even looked up. She was wearing tight pink trousers with little slits above the ankles and pointed shoes that were open at the back, more like slippers than pumps, pink too; besides that also a white blouse with long collar tips, and her lips were a deeper and shinier red than the paint on new Matchbox cars. She quickly stuck her tongue out at me.

But my father shook his head. 'I'm not taking you like that. Put something on first, please.'

'Why? It's more than 30 degrees . . .'

He turned a page. 'You know what I mean.'

A hint of red appeared in her face, and she looked down her front. 'Oh, can one see that?' Then she pulled the blouse tight, and now I also noticed that she wasn't wearing a bra. Once again she disappeared into her room.

It was so hot that it didn't feel as if we were out-side. The path through the gorse heath was asphalt, and seemed to lead directly to the mine's winding tower. The wheels were motionless, and the flag, at half mast, hung down limply. There was no breeze to stir the leaves on the trees, and no rustling in the dried-up grass. My father slung his jacket over his shoulder and said noth-ing. He never spoke much, and I couldn't think of any-thing to say either; I just plucked gorse blossoms off branches here and there and sucked on them. We used to imagine they were sweet; blossoms so yellow must be sweet. But they didn't taste of anything.

Marusha's heels clattered on the concrete, and she put on sunglasses and pointed to the horizon, where the contours of the mining plant seemed to be quiver-ing. White steam rose up from one of the cooling tow-ers, and the shadow of a crow darted overhead.

'Which one of those buildings do you work in, Herr Collien?'

The slim tie shone in the sun, a metallic brown. 'None of them. I work underground, just like your fa-ther.'

'Oh God. All day long?'

He nodded. 'All night long at the moment. Why?'

'I really don't get how people can do that. Isn't that unhealthy? The dirt, the dust, the bad air, and things always happen.'

'They do in other places too. On a building site you can fall off the scaffolding, and in a steelworks . . . well, whatever. The important thing is to feed the family, isn't it?' Marusha seemed to think about it, staring at the path. She scratched herself under her nose with her little finger.

'Well, probably . . .' Then she kicked away a crown cap, whistled silently to herself, and I stayed behind her, looking at her bottom in the tight trousers. Even squeezed my eyes together to see it better. But I couldn't make out the line of her knickers.

We turned off the bike path and went down across a narrow trail full of litter and rubble until we reached the pavement. It was Kleekampstrasse, the paved part where that still had house numbers. The housing blocks stood behind the bridge.

'God!' Marusha stopped and pushed the sunglasses up into her hair. 'Where are you taking me? I've never been here before!'

My father opened a wrought iron gate; it just about came up to his knees. There were countless flowers in the front garden, and every single blossom was like an explosion. There were a few yellow, white and orange ones, but most of them were red, and while my father rang the bell and we stood waiting, I took a look at Marusha's slip-ons. One could see the shape of her toes through the thin leather. She moved them slightly.

On the first floor a curtain was pulled a little to the side. An elderly woman. Her lips looked as if she had something bitter in her mouth. Then we heard someone coming down the stairs, and my father brushed a strand of hair from my forehead and pointed up with a roll of his eyes. 'He lives under the roof.'

We only saw that the amber-coloured door glass had a crack in it when a shadow covered it. The man who opened it was very gaunt, almost bony, and wasn't wearing any shoes, just socks. He was dressed in black, but the shirt didn't quite match the shade of the trousers. It looked new. There were gold threads woven into the collar and the cuffs, and he grinned broadly, almost mischievously, before shaking my father's hand.

'Wally, you old pit dog! Finally made it over here, eh?' His blonde hair was slightly messy, his eyes were blue, and he had a shaving cut on his chin. 'I knew something like that was on the cards. Got a few beers in the fridge. Come in, all o' ya!'

He held the door further open, but my father stayed where he was and put his hand on my shoulder. 'That's my eldest. Julian.'

'Hello!' He shook my hand with a firm grip and looked me straight in the face. Even the edges of his eyelids were black from coal dust. 'I'm Herbert. But you can call me Lippek, everyone does.'

'And this . . .'

'Well I'll be damned!' Still holding my hand with his right, he reached for Marusha's with his left. 'Didn't know you already had a grown-up daughter! That's a real trophy you've brought me.'

My father smiled sternly, and Marusha giggled and made an exaggerated curtsey. Then she introduced herself.

'Well.' Lippek smacked his lips and licked one corner of his mouth. He had a very big, sharply protruding Adam's apple. 'With so much beauty around we should talk proper, or we got no chance. So, up you go, keep going straight ahead until cloud nine. I'll just take a quick trip to the cellar. Got a tasty liqueur. Goes down like a dream.'

The stairwell smelled of polish. Pot plants on little stools were reflected in the reddish brown of the linoleum, and Marusha only touched the steps with the tips of her shoes. Sometimes her heels hit the brass rods like little hammers.

Lippek's apartment was tiny; there was a wardrobe standing on the landing in front of the door. He had a kitchen with a shower cabin, a narrow, windowless sleeping space and a living room where all the furniture was close together because of the roof pitches—a sofa with wooden armrests, a table with a yellowed lace cover under the glass top, and two cocktail armchairs. On a cupboard with shelves there were two rows of books, probably coffee-table books and a cardboard globe. The oceans on it were as blue as the sky in front of the open window.

'Sit down!' Lippek, slightly breathless, put an un-labelled bottle on the table. The liquid inside it looked like raspberry syrup, maybe a bit lighter. 'Beer's on the way.' Then he went to the kitchen, but turned round again in the doorway. I had sat down on an armchair, just on the edge, and tilted my head to read the book titles. 'For you I've got malt beer. Or lemonade.'

'Malt beer would be good, thanks.'

My father and Marusha sat down on the sofa. The light grey wallpaper, which looked as if the lines on it had been drawn by hand—it had a pattern of brushes, palettes and little picture frames—was darker and grease-stained behind their heads. There was flypaper hanging under the lamp, and the glue was already starting to run from the heat; it was clinging to the paper in brown drops.

Lippek put three bottles of beer and one of malt beer on the table and opened the cupboard as far as the armchairs allowed. He reached into the crack and took out glasses, beakers and a few bast mats. Then he uncorked the liqueur. 'Looks like our Sunday'll turn out nicely after all . . . ladies first.'

But my father held his fingers over Marusha's glass. She gasped and puffed up her cheeks in outrage, and Lippek frowned. 'What's up? Pregnant?'

She gave a laugh, but immediately put a hand in front of her mouth, just the fingertips. My father moved her beaker away. 'Nothing for her. At least, no spirits. She's 15, for God's sake!'

Lippek raised his eyebrows in amazement, but it looked acted. 'Seriously? I don't believe it. Good thing you told me. After all, you want to know what you're in jail for, right? And I thought she was already marriage-able.' He winked at her and filled the other glasses. It smelled of black currants. 'But she can have *one*, Wally. Can't she? Just for a toast. A bit of liquid fruit . . .'

My father looked at Marusha; I suppose he was ex-pecting her to turn it down herself. But she just pursed her lips, and Lippek poured her a beaker.

'So, ladies and gentlemen . . .' He lifted his glass. 'Nice to have you here.' He looked at me over his elbow and nodded at me. 'That's some father you've got! You know that? You couldn't have a better one. Nobody works as hard as him. But he's a real mate too. There . . .' He pointed to the slanted window niche with his chin. Under a little brass miner's lamp hung a hewer's certificate in an unvarnished wooden frame. My father had one just like it, but he kept it on his bedside table. 'I owe it all to him that I got anywhere in that old pit. Here's to our Wally the Wonder. Cheers!'

The men downed their liqueur, but Marusha just sipped hers. 'Mmh!' she said, running her tongue along her upper lip. 'It's not as sweet as I thought. Tastes great!'

'Great doesn't even begin to describe it.' Lippek filled the beer glasses. 'Here. Something to wash it down, then the next one.'

My father lit a cigarette and laid the packet on the table, the lighter on the packet, and pushed them both next to the ashtray. 'Are you doing the early shift tomorrow?'

He nodded.

'Who with?'

'No idea. Probably Motzkat.'

'Ah, you're lucky then. Have you fixed the plough on the fifth level yet? They can't even print health insurance certificates as fast as that thing shoots rocks everywhere. Mulisch told me you asked for a patented 50 millimetre tube?'

'Well he's got shit for brains, hasn't he! How can I ask for a 50 when we've only got a 30 connector! Don't believe everything that Dutch fool tells you.'

Marusha took another sip of her liqueur. Then she drank up and pushed the beaker over to our host. It was red from her lipstick. 'So is it true that you were a diamond robber, Mr Lippek?'

He stopped and shook his head. 'Now listen here ...' He aimed the neck of his bottle at her. 'Before you even say another word: this is my home, right? That's my name on the door, isn't it?' Marusha, shocked, nodded almost imperceptibly, but didn't say anything. She nibbled at her thumb. 'Well then! And in my home, you understand, there's no *Mister* anything. Even if the bailiff turned up, I'd say: listen mate, if you're sticking your seal on the fridge, you can bring me a beer too!'

She giggled, and he uncorked the bottle with his teeth. 'So, to you I'm Lippek. I'll come over to you in a minute, then we can seal it with a kiss. Everything has to be done correctly.'

Then he poured another round of liqueur, one for her too, and my father clicked his tongue quietly. 'Cut it out, man! That's already her second.'

Lippek nodded. 'Wally, I know you can count. And I don't mind if you count the props and caps for me either. You're the boss. But this here is my turf. Cheers!'

Marusha raised her glass, but unlike the others, she didn't drink this time. She put it back down on the table, took a sip of her beer and pointed to the packet of HB lying between the bottles. 'Do you want to treat me to one?'

Lippek wiped his mouth. 'I'd treat you to anything. But only if I can light it too.'

'Sure! Or d'you think I'd smoke it dry?'

I had gradually poured all the malt beer into my glass. It was now full to the brim, without any froth, and I leaned forward slowly to drink some off the top.

'So tell us then!' Marusha knocked on the table and took the lit cigarette. 'Did you steal some diamonds?'

He clicked his tongue quietly, looked at my father and motioned to the girl with his head. 'Would you believe it? I mean, that a girl like that's only 15? Incredible, isn't it? A real woman, take a look at her. Fully trained.'

'No.' I wiped up the beer with the tissue. 'She's still a trainee.'

He just shook his head, looked past the table at her legs. 'What's a woman like that still got to learn . . .'

She straightened her trouser crease and blew the smoke out very elegantly through her nose. 'Clothes saleswoman. At Kaiser und Gantz.'

'Oh my God! Seriously? I once bought some underpants there. That was embarrassing, I can tell you. This lady comes up to me, dressed up to the nines, and asks: "What crotch size've you got?" In front of everyone! And I say: "Er . . . don't know. Never measured it. A metre or so." And everyone looked at me like I was barmy.'

Marusha laughed, slapping her knees quickly several times. 'I bet that was Frau Niedl. She asks things like that. Was she called Niedl?'

He scratched the back of his neck. 'How should I know what the tart's name was. I'm sticking to the bargain counter in future, I can tell you that.'

He twisted the cork out of the bottle again and looked at me. He had big hands too, though the wrists were surprisingly delicate. 'Well, you're a quiet one! Like your old man, eh? Getting you two to talk is like pulling teeth. What d'you want to be?'

I grinned, shrugged my shoulders, and my father put out his cigarette. 'He's good at drawing.'

'Is that right? Well, I suppose we need some of that too. Then he won't be stupid enough to get a job in the pit, will he? If my son came to me and said: "listen, I want to be a miner"—I'd stick the shovel in his back.'

My father gave a little snort. 'You haven't even got kids!'

Lippek refilled. 'So what? What difference does that make? It doesn't make any difference. Who knows what the future holds in store.' He raised his beaker with two fingers like a chess piece and clinked it against Marusha's glass. 'Come on, sweetie, you're behind. Down with it!'

She tapped her forehead, and my father also made a defensive hand movement. 'Stop it now, Herbert. In this heat . . . what d'you think Konrad'll say if I bring her home sloshed.'

'Gorny? I've had the odd drink with him too. He's just as much of a lightweight as she is. Cheers, mate!'

He clinked glasses with him—but now Marusha grabbed her liqueur too. She threw her head back so abruptly that her sunglasses slipped out of her hair. The look on her face stayed exactly the same; she just closed her eyes briefly once, then put down the beaker before the men did. Her cheeks glowed.

My father looked at her the way he sometimes

RALF ROTHMANN

looked at Sophie; very strictly, but with a certain sadness in his eyes, and she lifted her shoulders.

'So what? I'm turning 16. And I don't care what Gorny says. He's not my father.' Then she brushed off the ash and turned to Lippek again. 'So tell us! Were you really in on that diamond robbery? With guns and everything?'

'Not him!' I spoke half into my glass. 'That was his brother.'

Lippek poured out some more beer, and foam dripped onto the table. He turned round and frowned. 'What about my brother?'

The look on his face didn't quite match the head movement, and he seemed to be speaking with a bit more effort. My father pushed his Gold-Dollar to him across the table. 'I told him about the robbery. It was in the papers anyway.'

The other man nodded. 'Sure. You can tell them. They're all idiots, thick as pigshit. Now they're rotting away in jail somewhere.' He pulled a cigarette out of the box and pointed it at Marusha. 'Diamonds aren't worth anything, let me tell you. Not worth the dirt under my nails. The woman who marries me doesn't need diamonds. What's she supposed to do with them anyway? She can't heat the house with them. But she'll always have a cellar full of coal, if you know what I mean. She'll always get a light!'

My father had both his hands on the table and was turning a mat about between his fingers. It was very fibrous, almost like hair. 'Diamonds are just coal anyway.'

Marusha put out her cigarette. 'What do you mean?'

'Well, they're made of carbon, just like any briquette. Except millions of years older.'

Lippek nodded thoughtfully. 'And you mustn't forget the pressing, Wally. It's like in life. If you press a woman the right way, she'll sparkle like a jewel.' He gave me a nudge with his toes. 'Isn't that right?'

Then he stood up, maybe a bit too abruptly; he had to prop himself up against the cupboard. He reached onto the shelf and held out an illustrated book: *The Western Second Division, 1947–1963*. Black and white. 'Well, how's that? It's got everything in it, all the matches with the team set-ups, the most important goals, the nicest fouls.' His hand trembled slightly as he turned the pages for me; his yellow fingernails were cut, but not filed. 'Look over here, old Kuzorra, Helmut Rahn, and there—Horst Szymaniak. He's from Erken-schwick, just like me. You can have it.'

'Thanks!' I put it on my lap, and my father gave me a surprised look and loosened his tie.

'But you're not even interested in soccer, are you?' He spoke a bit more slowly than usual, and his forehead and cheekbones had an unpleasant shine to them. I shrugged my shoulders and looked out of the window.

'What?!' Lippek sat down again. 'Wally's son's not interested in sport? You can't be serious.' He uncorked the liqueur and poured a glass. 'I just can't believe it. What sort of lad are you?'

My father took the beaker. 'He's good at drawing. Once I had to go to school because his teacher couldn't believe that he'd drawn a swallow's nest all by himself. He'd even put in those tiny little hairs around the nostrils.'

Marusha looked around. 'Don't you have any music?'

'Course I do!' Lippek motioned with his head. 'Right next to you, the whole box is full. But don't turn it up so loud, or I'll have the old dragon after me. I still owe her last month's rent.'

She bent over an armrest of the couch and folded out a cupboard door. Her blouse tightened, and I could see her bra. It was a delicate white. She took a few records off the stand and put them on the ten-record changer. But on the first song the pick-up arm sank down onto the turntable, its grooved surface, and I changed the speed from 33 to 45. *Men are ten a penny, and there are oh-so-many.*

'Oh God! Don't you have anything modern? Beatles or Lords?'

'Who? Me?' Lippek raised his glass. 'Is my name Pillek or something? I'm not having nigger music like that in my house. Isn't that right, Wally? More beer?' He looked at me. 'Can you go to the fridge? In the veg compartment . . .'

I stood up. The kitchen was small; there was just one chair at the square table with its chrome-plated steel-bar legs. The tear-off calendar was still on May.

A shirt was dripping on a wire hanger in the shower cabin, and the light in the fridge didn't work. But there was a thick chunk of ice stuck to the freezer.

Underneath there was only a jar of gherkins and a plate with a half-eaten piece of brawn and a few fried potatoes; the fork was still on the plate. I took two bottles of beer out of the bottom drawer and brought them to the living room.

'That's really a good boy you've got.' Lippek already had the opener in his hand; it had a lacquered bamboo handle, and my father, both his arms on the backrest of the sofa, shrugged his shoulders. His eyes were already slightly glazed. 'Just a bit quiet,' Lippek added, opening the bottles.

'Still waters run deep.' Marusha smirked, and with a smack a new record fell onto the turntable. *White Roses From Athens*.

My father nodded. 'Out in the country he was different. A real wild one. He was already babbling our ears off before he could even talk. And always up to no good.'

I moved around a bit in my armchair, opening the book and shutting it again. Crossed my legs.

'Once, he was about two . . .'

'Dad!' I turned away slightly. 'Not again! We know that one.'

He shook his head. 'You know it. They don't. So,

he was still little, and we bought him a red knitted play-suit, one of those one-piece things you button up.'

Marusha clicked her fingers. 'They're called over-alls.'

'Whatever. Anyway, we went out one evening to milk the cows, and he toddled after us as always. Then it started raining, and I told him: "Sit down there under the trailer!" So he did what he was told, and played somewhere by the milk churns. We did our work, of course, like in any weather, and didn't watch him for a while. Next time we looked, we couldn't believe our eyes. He'd found the milking grease and covered himself in the stuff from head to toe! He looked like a piece of butter, I tell you. And of course that was the end of his expensive playsuit.'

Marusha giggled, sipped her liqueur, and Lippek grinned too. 'A bit of body care, eh? Nothing wrong with that.' He stretched out a leg into the table's shadow, and for a moment I thought I could smell his feet. But maybe it was mine, I was only wearing sandals.

'And one time . . .' My father ran his fingers through his hair; he had big sweat patches under his arms. I reached for my glass. But it was empty.

'Dad, please!'

He took no notice of me. He looked up at the lamp as if he were dreaming, and Lippek touched Marusha's foot. She had slipped out of her shoes a while ago, and didn't recoil. But looked at my father as if she was hanging onto his every word.

He moved his head. 'You couldn't even take your eyes off him for five minutes. We had a paddock, it was pretty stony. Little gravel heaps everywhere, and the boy was crawling about between the cows. They were impatient, waiting to be milked. They were roaring and stamping. But he crawled through under them on all fours, babbling and singing, and what he liked most of all was rubbing his little head against their teats.'

Marusha pulled one foot onto the sofa and folded her hands in front of her knee. But she left the other one under the table, and Lippek's toes, in his black socks, glided over the instep with a movement that reminded me of a caterpillar.

'I just can't imagine that you used to live in the country, Wally. Really can't imagine it.'

My father nodded, turned his head and looked up at the sky, which was still cloudless. 'And suddenly he found out that he could pull himself up if he held on to a cow's tail. Which he did. And then he bent down to pick up the pebbles lying between the rear hooves, then took them one after another and stuck them in the cow's hole.'

Marusha put her hand in front of her mouth, but she seemed to be grinning behind her fingers. Lippek took a swig from the bottle.

'In which one?'

My father shook his head. 'The arsehole, of course. The other one's shut when they're not in heat. He pushed in one pebble after another, I don't know how many. My wife and me, we stopped milking and had a look. Some of the stones were as big as table tennis balls, and he put them on the groove made by the sphincter muscle, pushed with the flat of his hand, and—plop—they were gone. That went on for five minutes or so; we almost wet ourselves laughing. And the little lad had a look on his face as if he was doing some really serious work.'

'And then?' Marusha crossed her arms in front of her chest as if she were cold. At the same time she tilted her foot, allowing Lippek to touch the sole.

My father drank some beer. 'Well, after a while I suppose it'd had enough. We heard a sort of rumbling and clicking inside the cow, it turned its head and roared, and then—plop, plop—it shat them all out again. And our boy was standing next to it, clapping his hands.'

Marusha took a Gold-Dollar without asking. Her eyes were glowing too, and her speech was slightly slurred. 'So that's what you're like? A dirty one, aren't you!'

I grinned, but my father frowned and pushed his lighter over to her. 'What's dirty about that? For a child?'

'But really . . .' Lippek burped with his cheeks puffed out. 'I just can't get my head round it that *you* were such a country bumpkin, mister foreman. You're a digger! You belong underground!'

While he drank the rest of his beer, his big toe glided across the sole of Marusha's foot, very gently, and she opened her mouth and brushed one of her chestnut-coloured curls behind her ear. I could see her nipples under the blouse.

My father rubbed the back of his neck. He was speaking more laboriously now, less clearly too, with pauses between sentences, and staring in front of him. 'He was just curious. I was exactly the same at that age. I crawled into every nook I found too. Like a little dog. The chicken coop, for example. And then I came out screaming with a rooster on my head, a little Leghorn rooster. It had dug its claws into my hair and was pecking at me like crazy. As if I wanted to steal his hens.'

I clicked my fingers and pointed at his wrist. But he didn't react.

'And one time it was really bad. Hardly bears thinking about. Besides farms there was also a little stud farm, standardbred racehorses. And one of the mares, a lovely brown one, was a real wild beast. You just couldn't curb her—at least not when she had a foal. Didn't let anyone near her, except for the squire's wife. She shattered one stable hand's pelvis, and she bit and kicked the other horses till they bled. So she and her foal got a paddock of their own.'

Marusha had pulled her foot away from Lippek. Neither of them seemed to be listening to my father anymore. They were looking at each other, but as if staring through chiffon. Their reflections on the tabletop met where the almost empty liqueur bottle was standing, and our host wobbled slightly in his seat. My father plucked a piece of fluff off his shirt.

'She knew what she was worth. And one day . . .'

I cleared my throat exaggeratedly, waved one of the mats, pointed to his watch again, and now he looked up, strangely dazed. His eyes, which suddenly had dark rings around them, seemed further back in their sockets, and he nodded and pushed his cuff back.

'What's up?' Lippek sat up. 'Are you getting unsociable on me? Now don't make me faint!'

My father turned the knob on his watch. 'The boy's right, Herbert. I still need a portion of shuteye. Have to start my shift soon.'

'What?' Marusha also seemed surprised. 'But it's Sunday!'

He put away the cigarettes and the lighter. 'Not down there . . .' When he got up he almost banged his head on the lamp, the yellow glass bowls that looked like berets. There was a coin lying in one of them.

'But then we should at least have one for the road!' Lippek quickly filled the beakers. 'Fruit's good for you.' Marusha had also stood up, and he handed both of them their glasses, filled to the brim; the liqueur ran down his fingers and dripped onto the carpet. He swayed and rested a hand on my shoulder, and I stiffened to prop him up. 'So, friends: one, two, three, and down the hatch!'

With the glass at her lips, Marusha snorted and looked at me. She was holding her shoes in one hand, and when the three of them had drunk and put the beakers on the table one after another, it sounded like her stilettos on the stairs. The flowers seemed to glow in the light.

'Those are dahlias.' Our shadows glided across them. When we got to the end of the garden path, my father stopped and tightened his tie again. 'We had even more in the old days. They grow like wildfire.'

The other two had stayed slightly behind, talking to each other in the gloomy hallway, where it smelled of coffee and homemade cake, and I stepped up to my father and asked him, almost whispering:

'So what did his brother do with the diamonds?'

He crushed a petal between his fingers. 'No idea. They were rough diamonds, and you'll never sell those. Not on the black market. And nobody'll cut stolen diamonds for you, at least no professional. I think the whole thing was a flop.'

233

Marusha gave a laugh—a bright, tipsy laugh with a snoring sound at the end, but my father didn't turn round. He was looking over to the other side of the road, where there was a garden full of dwarves. One of them was reading a book. His friend put an arm around the girl, smelling her hair. 'And when?'

Marusha grinned. 'We'll see . . .'

He touched her again, tried to reach under her arm for her breast, but she pushed him away, and my father opened the gate. One of the other dwarves looked as if he used to be holding a cup, but only the handle was left now. On the pavement we turned round, and Lippek, his shirt hanging out of his trousers, waved. 'Good luck!' Marusha blew him a kiss.

Then we turned off onto the narrow, slightly rising path. I was the last, and Marusha kept holding the gorse branches so that they wouldn't hit me in the face. The asphalt on the bike path was soft now, her heels left prints, and my father hummed quietly, which he rarely did—probably never. It almost sounded like a fountain. I couldn't make out the tune.

'Hey!' Marusha straightened her blouse and put her sunglasses on. 'I'm the woman, I have to go in the middle!' But when she linked arms with us, my father fell silent and looked over to the cooling tower. She smelled a bit sweaty, but it was perfumed sweat, and I breathed deeply. Little pearls on the end of her nose too.

'D'you like Lippek?'

'Him?' She smiled gently, almost pityingly. 'You must be joking! He drinks too much. And he's too small for me. One wants someone to lean on, you understand. If he was like your father . . .'

He shook his head. 'What are you talking about? Herbert's just as tall as me.'

'But you seem bigger. Because you're calmer.'

'What a load of rubbish!' It sounded strict, and he seemed to be making an effort to suppress a smile as he said it. But one could still see it.

Marusha skipped. 'Shall we sing?'

'What?!' I pulled my arm away, and my father didn't even answer. He lit a cigarette. The smoke hardly seemed to move in the hot afternoon air. The motorway shimmered on the horizon.

Marusha put on her sulky pout. There was lipstick only in the corners of her mouth now. 'All right then, we won't. And who knows some jokes?'

No one answered. I picked at the twigs, and she looked up at my father. 'Wow, you two are real party animals, aren't you. But then you have to finish the story with the horse. You know—that vicious mare . . .'

'God, no! I'll tell a joke.'

'Oh yeah? Let's hear it.'

I thought for a moment. 'A long one or a short one?'

'A funny one.'

'All right . . . A man's got a huge library. Then the woman from next door comes and says: "You've got great books. Could I borrow one?" "Sure," says the man, "but you have to read it here." He said that because he'd often lent out books and not got them back.'

Marusha put a hand to her neck and loosened her collar.

'And that's it?'

'Now wait a minute. A few days later he sees her with a new lawnmower and says: "What a great lawnmower! Can I borrow it?" "Sure," says the woman, "but you have to mow here."'

She giggled, but I couldn't see her eyes behind her sunglasses, and my father, who probably hadn't even been listening, ran his fingers through my hair quickly. I felt the cufflink against my ear. And then he cleared his throat and started after all . . .

'Luna was her name, the moon. The very thought of it . . . nobody could go into the paddock. You really would've been risking your life. The fence bordered our garden, with a warning sign on every corner, and one day we didn't watch her for a bit. We were hoeing in the vegetable patch, and suddenly we heard her snorting. My wife nudged me. She was as white as a sheet. "Oh my God," she said. "The boy!" He'd crawled in under the wire and was toddling over to the mare, and I was just about to shout "Juli! Get back!" But that would only have given the animal a shock and made it even more dangerous. It was already scratching away at the ground and staring wildly at him, and the foal jumped away and fled to the other end of the paddock. So we went up to the fence and called him quietly. But he squatted down, picked a few mushrooms, and for a moment I was thinking about running over and grabbing him. But he was already too close to the mare—though she hadn't flattened her ears back yet, oddly enough. Her tail was flailing about, but she just stood there and looked at my son. And he had no idea of fear.

He laughed and babbled "Lunaluna," holding the stupid mushrooms out to her. She knocked them out of his hand with her snout, but didn't bite him, and my wife dug her fingers into my arm and said: "Do something! For God's sake, come on!" But what was I supposed to do? If I'd gone into the paddock, the animal would have bucked and kicked in all directions. But at the moment it was calm. It bent down its neck and sniffed Juli from head to toe, and he laughed and fingered her nostrils. And when Luna gave him a push, he fell on his nappy bum and screeched with delight.'

Marusha pulled the cigarette from between his fingers, dragged on it and gave it back. Then she put her arm in mine again.

'Meanwhile all the neighbours had gathered round, the pig boy, the maid from the manor, and even the baker had got out of his bread van and gone up to the fence. And they all called out: "Juli, come! Juli, chocolate!" My wife even waved his teddy. But the little lad didn't even seem to hear us. He crawled about under the mare while she stayed completely still and looked around for the foal. The foal plucked up its courage and slowly came closer, sniffed at my son, and Liesel called out again: "Come, Juli! Please come!" But he pulled himself up by a hind leg and just said "No." He didn't even turn round. Just: "No!" And then he started stroking the animal.'

Marusha looked at me, shaking her head. There was something cheeky about her smile.

'Can you imagine it!' My father breathed deeply. 'While the foal's drinking, he's standing between this devil mare's massive hind legs and stroking her coat, the lighter part on the inside of the thighs. It's particularly smooth and soft there; God knows how he found that out. And all the while saying: "There there, Luna, there there." And happy as a king.'

'And the mare?'

'She didn't move an inch. She seemed to like it. So now the foal's long gone to the other end of the paddock, chasing butterflies, and the mother lets him stroke her—I don't know how long that went on. I still get goose pimples when I think of that endless "there, there." '

He flicked the cigarette onto the asphalt, and I stamped it out. 'But after a while I suppose she'd had enough, and took a step forwards. My little lad fell over, screamed with shock, and everyone held their breath. Because the mare got a shock too, and was standing a bit askew. To find her footing again, she would have had to put her hoof exactly where the boy was lying. But she lifted it carefully over him, snorted—and followed the foal to the lower part of the paddock.'

'Phew,' said Marusha, undoing another button on her blouse. 'I would've died three times. As a mother, I mean.'

My father grinned. 'Liesel was shaking like a leaf. I can tell you . . .' He looked at me. 'I think that was the day you got your first real thrashing, eh?'

'Really?' I went in front, grabbing for a fly. 'Maybe. I can't remember, can I?'

When we were home again, on the landing, Marusha gave me a clap. 'Well then, you two . . . that was a nice outing. Next time it's my turn.' She opened her door. 'And now I'll hit the hay for an hour or two.' But she turned round again on the doorstep and pointed at my father, who was pulling at his shoelaces. They seemed to have got tangled up. 'Are *you* going to make his sandwiches? Or shall I . . . ?'

'What?' I slipped out of my sandals. 'Why should you?'

She shrugged her shoulders, and by the time he straightened up again she was almost in her room. He looked pale and tired, and wiped his feet on the mat; but he was holding his shoes in his hand. The tie was loose.

'Brush your teeth when you go down, you hear. So they don't smell your breath. Or they'll say I got you drunk.'

She smiled in a strange, almost sad way. 'But you did.' Then she closed the door.

I got changed, and when I came back from the toilet, my father's shirt and trousers were lying on the bed. Holding an issue of *Bild*, he was standing in front of the TV in his underwear and watching a game of soccer. He wobbled slightly, and I went into the kitchen and pulled the lid off the sausage box. 'When are you going?'

'A bit later today. It's just a short shift. Why?'

'Could I take your bike? I want to go for a swim in the quarry pond. I'll be back in time, I promise.'

'All right.' He turned off the TV. 'But don't run over any shards.'

The road to Kirchhellen was new—there were no markings on the asphalt yet—and the firm tyres hardly made a sound. Riding in wavy lines with no hands, I ate a corned beef sandwich. Then I leaned far out over the handlebars, bent my elbows and let out a piercing shriek as I passed the fence of the chicken farm. But the animals didn't move, they just carried on dozing in their holes.

Shortly before Grafenmühle, the end of the road, I turned off onto the stony path leading to the pit, where the sun made the greyish-brown spruce trees high above look almost golden. There wasn't even a hint of a breeze to stir their dusty tops. A lot of cars were parked around the lake, as always at the weekend, and I heard the noise of the radios and the calling and screaming of the bathing guests a long way off. Someone was playing the trumpet.

I bought a bottle of Sinalco from the ice cream man in the three-wheeler and rode around the car park. The path, with lots of tree roots growing through it, led to the smaller lake that couldn't be accessed by car anymore. Half of it was overgrown with reeds; one normally had peace and quiet there. As I reached the clearing in front of the bathing part, Zorro leapt towards me. He was soaking wet and howling with joy, though his left hind leg kept giving way; I leaned the bike against a spruce tree and scratched his coat. The Marondes were in the water up to their stomachs, and the air mattress between them had all sorts of things lying on it—a dented cooking pot, a shovel blade full of holes, tin cans, handlebars. I waved at them, pulled my blanket off the carrier and went to the shore, where Fattie was lying, stark naked. He was leafing through a magazine and didn't respond to my 'Hello', hardly looked up. He sniffed.

'Hey, Juli!' Karl had squatted down, the water now came up to his neck, and I spread out my blanket. He lifted up an old steam iron, covered in moss. 'Go away, Juli! It's August now, not July!'

'Very funny . . .' I got undressed, rolled my clothes up into a pillow, and opened the book I had brought: *The Leatherstocking Tales*. Zorro lay down next to me in the grass. He smelled slightly brackish, like the lake.

Fattie looked up. 'What's all this? You can't lie here like that. This is a nudist beach.'

'Oh really?' I stared at the page, but didn't read. 'Since when?'

'Always has been. Or do you see any swimming trunks here?'

I pointed at the dog, but Fattie didn't grin. He scratched his balls. Franz and Karl pulled the mattress to the shore. They weren't wearing anything either, and they already had lots of hair. They threw the scrap metal they had fished from the bottom into the bushes, and Fattie clicked his fingers.

'Come over here and look at shorty. Doesn't he look like a nancy boy in his latex bag?'

The other two looked round and eyed me up. Karl's left forearm was still swollen from the tattoo he had made himself, a heart struck by lightning, and Franz wiped his hands on his bottom and came towards me. He was squinting a bit, and as he stood over me, water dripped from his body onto my book, onto the jacket I had made out of newspaper.

'Hey!' I slid to the side. 'Watch it!' But he shook the water out of his hair over me, his penis dangling about—while his brother approached with a handful of duckweed. I leapt up. Fattie turned the page.

'So, either get your kit off, or piss off. We cleaned up the shore, and we say who bathes here and how.'

I didn't say anything. I got my things together, and Karl rubbed the green stuff into Zorro's coat, which he seemed to enjoy; he jumped up at his calves. I walked along the track that went around the lake until I reached the next spot where one could get to the water without having to go through the reeds. But there was a small ditch in the long grass, and when I lay down in it, all I could see was the sky and the treetops full of pine cones. Though I couldn't feel any breeze, they were moving very slightly.

I drank my lemonade in small sips and read for a while. I hardly heard any sounds from the others except an occasional splash or laugh, and one time a fart. With the book on my chest, I dozed in the sun. It was low, and my body was full of insect bites. I had scratched some of the wounds open again without noticing, but when the buzzing of mosquitoes above me got louder than the distant sounds of the bathers at the big lake, I sat up. The newspaper came off the book, and the sand-coloured binding was lighter where there was an advertisement: Trill pet food. The dark picture of a guinea pig must have kept off the sun.

When I went down to the water, the other bathing spot was empty. No trace of Zorro either. The grass was

still flat where the blanket had lain, a crumpled cigarette packet lay next to it, charred matches too, and I
shielded my eyes with my hand to see better. But it was
clear enough: the bike was gone.

I took my things, ran through the ferns and called
Fattie, several times; but there was no one in the trees.
There was a roll of wire in the moss, a sign with
'Forestry Office' written on it, shot to pieces, a shoe,
and I scoured the undergrowth by the shore, looked in
the reeds and even waded into the water, which was a
murky green. One could hardly see more than a few
inches down into the water, and I swore quietly,
clenched my teeth and ploughed through the mud at
the bottom with my feet. I didn't even think of shards.
But the only thing my feet knocked against was an old
moped wheel, its spokes full of algae.

Then I got dressed and walked to the big lake,
which had now almost been covered by the evening
shadows. There was only one car left there, a Ford
Taunus with its doors open. I heard a radio, and there
were two couples lying on big blankets, snogging and
fondling each other. Empty beer bottles had been stuck
neck-down into the sand, the golden ears of wheat on

the labels shone in the sun, and one of the men cast a quick loop up at me when my shadow fell on them.

'Excuse me, have you seen three boys with four bikes? There was a dog too. They robbed me, and I have to . . .'

'Hop it, shorty.' The man, who had long curly hair and a moustache, looked the woman in the eyes. She was wearing a bikini, and he stroked her stomach, plucking a piece of fluff out of her navel. 'You're bothering us.'

'I know. But maybe you can help me? The bike was only borrowed. It's my father's, and he needs it to get to work! Right now! I mean, what am I supposed to do . . .'

No one reacted. The other couple was kissing with their mouths wide open. Their cheeks curved inwards. The curly-haired man pushed his fingertips under the hem of the woman's bikini panties and she closed her eyes; I turned away and walked along the track to the road where there were a few rabbits sitting motionless. The asphalt was warm. The sun was shining somewhere behind the poplars that marked the borders of the fields on the horizon, and I cupped my hands around my mouth, but then didn't know which direction I should call in. I started running.

With the book in one hand, I held the corners of the blanket I had hung over my shoulders together under my chin; that way it was easier to carry. And while it flapped about behind me I listened to the rhythm of my steps, the slapping of the sandals against the bluish-black surface, and shouted at myself whenever I slowed down. A few cars drove past me, but none of them were heading in my direction.

The courtyard between the shacks on the chicken farm was empty, only shadows in the burrows, and the late afternoon light made the fluff on the wire fence look even whiter. I had to sneeze when I ran past it. On the pastures on either side of the dead straight road there were a few cows standing around the water tanks, and the streetlamps on the motorway bridge went on. There was a family leaning on the railing, waving to the passing trucks.

As the sun went down below the coal heaps, I turned off onto the estate. Our house was dark, at least on the street side, and I dashed up the stairs two steps at a time; my knees almost gave way on the last few.

Marusha was standing on the doorstep of her room with an open powder tin in her hands. A brush was pointing out of her dressing gown pocket, and she shook her head.

'He was fuming, I can tell you!' She smirked strictly, eyeing my bite-covered legs. 'You can thank your lucky stars my bike didn't have a flat tyre . . .'

I couldn't speak, and was about to unlock the door, but found that it was only ajar. Wheezing, I propped myself against the couch table. The apartment was dark and empty, and smelled of soap or aftershave. My father's cigarette packet lay on the stool, the lighter on the packet, and it was only now, while slowly catching my breath, that I started crying. There was nothing I could do to stop it. My tears fell onto the newspaper.

Later on I had some bread and jam, drank a cup of peppermint tea and watched TV. On the first channel they were showing one of those films where American women rush down very long flights of stairs and throw their arms around a man who's just about to go to war. Or coming back from one. On the other channel there were two old men talking. One of them was a fat, bald-headed man wearing a tie, the other was thinner and pretty nervous. He was sweating like anything and smoking one cigarette after another; the ashtray next to the microphone on the table was full of butts. Whenever the fat man asked him a question he pointed at him with two fingers together, and the other one kept nodding while he listened, sometimes fiddling with his collar. He spoke with a Cologne accent, had big, dark eyes that somehow seemed bright, and his nose was slightly knobbly. He almost looked like a sad clown. But he must have been a writer, because one time the interviewer said: 'And you, as an author of modern novels and short stories, seriously believe . . .' I didn't understand what they were talking about, not a word. But the look on the man's face, his constant sweating—drops were falling from his chin onto his chest—and the almost timid, or at least restrained, yet still resolute way in which he answered was fascinating to me: I moved the armchair right up to the screen, intent on finding out his name so that I could look him up in the parish library. But his name wasn't mentioned, at least not for as long as I could keep my eyes open.

I turned off the TV and went into my room, opened the window. My feet were burning from the long run, and I took off my shirt, trousers and the tight swimming trunks and crawled into bed. Behind Fernewaldstrasse I heard the rumbling of the freight train and the long whistling of the locomotive that chased playing children off the tracks in the daytime, and at night deer and rabbits that had frozen in the light of the headlamps. Then I fell asleep.

But I kept waking up because the bites were itching so much. I wiped spit on them. Later on I dreamt about my mother, who was sick and lying on an air mattress. She drifted out to sea, and I dived into the water head-first to save her. But the murky water was shallow; I scraped my chest and legs on stones and came up again, feeling as if I'd been skinned.

The next time I opened my eyes I still had one of the writer's phrases in my ear: 'silent immunity'. I didn't know what it was or what context he had mentioned it in; and it didn't matter. I liked the sound. There was something eternally comforting in it when he said: 'There is a silent immunity against that.'

Then I looked at the alarm clock, and for a moment I thought it had stopped; hardly any time had passed. But it was ticking. I'd left the curtains open, and the moon was shining directly onto my bed. I kicked away the bedclothes and scratched myself with both hands, getting faster and faster.

Something rumbled in the house, probably on the ground floor. Scabs under my nails. Then someone giggled, but it was probably a bird chirping somewhere in the garden, and I kneeled down on the bed and drew the curtains. The sparkle in the eyes of my sister's teddy bears and dolls disappeared, and now I saw that the clock's luminous hands didn't show quarter past 10, but rather 10 to three. I heard a mosquito, very close, and smacked my ear.

Something jammed above me. I pulled harder on the curtain, and suddenly the sound made by the wheels in the track seemed terrifying. I ducked down behind the plants. In the moonlight the garden looked as if it had been dusted with grey lime, and for the length of a heartbeat I thought it might be an illusion. There was no breeze to stir the leaves on the trees. A few appliances were propped up under the shed canopy, the shiny prongs of a rake shimmered out from the shadows, which were blacker than the night sky—and then Herr Gorny took a puff on his cigarette.

He reached behind him, closed the door and stepped into the light. I'd never noticed him smoking before; the glow of the embers coloured his chin while he walked about slowly between the trees, checking the rootstocks he'd set up a few days ago, the grafts. He was wearing a striped dressing gown, the same as my father's, and no pyjama trousers—at least not long ones. His pale calves stuck out under the hem, and his naked feet were in street shoes with their laces undone. While plucking a yellow leaf from a spider's thread he cast a quick look up the house, but more in the direction of our balcony, and frowned. He took another drag on his cigarette, threw it into the water butt, and walked along slowly with both hands in his pockets. Some of the trees were so small that they only came up to his chest, and sometimes he sniffed at the ones that had been grafted together, touched them. There was a blind reflection on his watch glass.

Smoke rose from the empty water butt, a slim thread, and I had almost finished darkening the room. The spout of the watering can pushed against the cloth like a nose, and I moved it back and carefully pulled the curtain further along—then it got stuck on a plant, as it did so often, a little cactus with small spines. The pot fell almost silently onto the ledge, and only a few crumbs of earth fell out. But the plate it was on rattled, and Herr Gorny looked up. I couldn't make out his eyes. Two dark hollows. But for him I must have looked as if I had a spotlight pointed at me, at least up to my chest. The moon was full, its delicate grey aura had a brownish outline, and I wobbled a little on my knees, holding on to the windowsill. The clock ticked loudly, then more quietly again as we stood motionless, looking at each other. The shadow of his chin went across his neck, his nose's went across his lips, and his hair, normally combed back neatly, stood up in every possible direction; finally he nodded at me. But I didn't react, not even when he seemed to smile. I looked for the cord with my fingers, its frayed tassel, and before I pulled the cloth in front of the window I saw Herr Gorny taking his hands out of his pockets and walking straight across the lawn to the house.

I put on my swimming trunks, missing one of the leg holes in the rush and banging my knee against the edge of the cupboard. My parents' bedroom was empty, of course. There was a Jerry Cotton book lying on my father's bed, and the bedspread on my mother's half looked like something metallic in the dressing table mirror. Or like the back of a big beetle. Limping, I ran to the living room, locked the door and put the key in the fruit bowl.

He must have come through the cellar; the hinges on the grate squeaked. He didn't turn on the light on the stairs; the crack under the door stayed black. Maybe he'd taken off his shoes, as I didn't hear any footsteps—just an occasional creak of the stairs, and only very quietly, as if he were coming up along the narrow inside.

I sat down on the sofa, put my folded hands between my knees, and breathed with my mouth open to avoid making any sound. When I heard the next creak I closed my eyes. My heart was beating so hard that it felt like someone was banging on my neck from the outside. My bowels rumbled; I needed the toilet.

But then I thought that maybe I hadn't locked the door properly in the rush, and I stood up, shivering with fear, and stretched out my hand. My fingers were trembling. The floorboards creaked again, the doormat knocked against the door, I smelled the aftershave, or imagined I did—and at the very moment I took hold of the door handle, I felt a tension in it from the other side and froze.

It was pushed down very slowly, and I breathed in sharply, the way one does when stepping into a bath that's too hot after thinking for a second that it was cold—The door was locked; the handle moved up and down several times. The moon—a glimmer, seemed to glide off it. I didn't react to the hissing and mumbling in the hall, but went backwards to the kitchen. There were plates and cutlery lying in the sink, and a kitchen knife with a wooden handle wobbled slightly as drops of water from the tap fell onto it, again and again. The balcony door was open, but Marusha's window was closed. No light.

But I still took a step through the doorway and knocked against the glass, a quick drumming with my fingertips that I hardly heard myself over the noise of a passing coal train, its rumbling under the bridges. But something was moving behind the window. I stood in the slanting shadow cast by the canopy and one side opened, just a crack at first; wheezing with relief, I tried to swallow my saliva, but couldn't. I couldn't see Marusha yet. She whispered something I didn't understand, pulled on the red cloth, and suddenly the moonlight was like a scream in the mirror. I squatted down and slid under the table. Where it smelled of my sister's chewing gum.

'So what?' Marusha giggled. 'It's fine. Hold on to this . . .'

A cornflake crumbled under my hand. Whatever was lying on the table was heavy; the wood bent slightly, the stilted legs creaked, and then I saw one foot on the chair and another one on the stone floor. The muscular calves were covered in little scars, black from the coal dust that had worked its way under the skin, and the two big toes were bent inwards just like mine. Hammer toes.

'Good night. See you tomorrow.'

My father's voice was also hushed. 'Wash yourself,' he said, went to the kitchen and opened the fridge. Stark naked, he was carrying his clothes over one arm and holding his shoes in his hand. After getting something out of the side compartment, probably a piece of cheese, he pushed the door shut again. He didn't notice me. He drank a mouthful of water from the tap and went to bed.

I couldn't sleep anymore. Cocks were crowing somewhere in Kleekamp, and the sun was still pretty low
when I slipped into my clothes and packed a few things
into my sports bag. Socks, underwear, *Oliver Twist*. Then
I filled some of the lentil soup Frau Gorny had cooked
us for the coming week into an old gherkin glass and
cut a slice of bread. Through the half-open door I saw
my father, covered only with a sheet. He was lying on his
stomach with one leg bent, and for a moment I thought
he was awake. But he was just grinding his teeth, as he
often did in his sleep. Then I pulled the door shut and
went down the stairs as quietly as I could.

My windcheater was still a bit too big for me; it
almost went down to the hems of my shorts. The fences
and hedges cast long shadows, dew sparkled in the grass.
Little Schulz was sitting on the balcony in his pyjamas
drinking something out of a big gold-edged cup. He had
put his cars on the railing one by one; there was a bread
roll lying on top of a semi-trailer truck, and he waved at
me. I waved back.

No bike in front of the Marondes' house, nor in
Fattie's garden, and I crossed Dorstener Strasse and
walked across the football field. Dust rose up from the
red gravel whenever I dragged my feet. On the other side

a man was pulling a rusty roller along the sidelines. In front of the wheels the line was faded, behind them a glowing white.

Reverend Stürwald looked at the clock when I entered the church. The morning light made the glass cross that hung from the dome by two wires shine in the colours of the rainbow. 'What's the matter with you?' He folded his sash together. 'No home to go to? It's ten to seven. And you're not even serving today, are you?'

'No. Only on Sunday again. But I want to confess.'

'Today? Confession is on Saturday, my boy.'

'But before early Mass too!'

'Sometimes. If anyone comes. But you can see: nobody here.'

'What do you mean? I'm here!'

He closed his eyes for a moment and sighed. Then he opened the door of the semicircular confessional; the rubber seal made a sucking sound as if there were a vacuum behind it. 'All right then, come on. Hurry up.'

I kneeled down on the cushioned bench, but left the curtain open. The priest put the sash on again and blessed me through the wire grille. He smelled of smoke.

I crossed myself. 'Bless me Father, for I have sinned. I have been disobedient, I have lied, I have stolen, and I have been unchaste. Amen.'

'Wait a minute, not so fast,' Stürwald whispered. 'What did you steal?'

'Well, I didn't really steal. I had it put on my parents' tab.'

'And what was it? Chocolate? Chewing gum? Trashy magazines?'

I shook my head. 'Beer and cigarettes. And a bottle of Doornkaat.'

He was silent for a moment. Then he leaned forward. 'Aha. And what did you do with all that?'

'Gave it away,' I said. 'You see, I wanted to stay a member of the animal club, and the others said . . .'

'Animal club?'

'Oh, just some kids' stuff. There are hardly any animals left anyway. But we even used to have a cockatiel. And a hunting dog, we've still got that. Its joints are a bit funny, but apart from that it's the real thing. And once the cat has had its kittens, there'll be more of us again.'

He cleared his throat; it sounded impatient. 'All right. And what was that about being unchaste?'

I gulped and said nothing for a while. He wound up his wristwatch, and it sounded as if the silence suddenly had little teeth.

'Come on now,' he insisted. 'How were you unchaste? Alone, or with someone else?'

'Me? Both.'

'And when you were unchaste with someone else— who started?'

'Started? Not me!'

'Was it a girl or a boy?'

'A girl.'

'And what did you do?'

'I don't know . . .'

'What do you mean, you don't know? Come on, do I have to drag every word out of you? Did you touch each other?'

'Yes, but we had our clothes on. She stroked my hand from the inside. And we kissed. I mean, I tried to kiss her. With my tongue.'

'Hm. And that was all?'

I didn't say anything, and he moved his folded fingers; the joints made a cracking sound. 'Well, maybe it's a little early, but that wasn't such an urgent reason for a confession. It could have waited until Saturday. You're getting to an age now when such things start happening more often, you know. But that's normal, and not everything is automatically a sin. The most important thing is not to lose sight of God because of it. What do we say in the Lord's Prayer? "And lead us not into temptation . . ." That's all very well, but the original version of the prayer is different: "And lead us in our temptation" . . . do you see the difference?'

'Hm . . .' I lowered my head and picked at my fingernails. People were coming into the church, I could hear the double doors squeaking. Someone coughed. But the priest moved closer to the grille, so close that I could see the hairs in his ears. And the dandruff on his shoulders. I cleared my throat. 'Herr Stürwald?'

'I'm listening, boy. I'm listening.'

'I've got a question. Or rather, a request. I mean, now that I've confessed to my sins—couldn't I confess for someone else too?'

'What do you want to do? For whom?'

'I can't tell you.'

'Why do you want to confess for someone else? He had best do that himself, hadn't he?'

'But he doesn't go to church. Ever.'

The priest shook his head. 'And you think you can simply . . . what has he done? Do you know his sins?'

'Yes. I think so.'

'And what are they?'

I took a breath. 'Well . . . he's a good person really. He never beats us, and he gives us money for lemonade and stuff like that. But he was unchaste too.'

'How do you know? Were you there?'

'Me? Goodness, no!'

He pulled at his ear. 'Now listen, my boy. Let me make one thing clear: no one can confess on another person's behalf. The person has to do that himself. For confession depends on repentance, as you know; otherwise it would be pointless. And you cannot repent someone else's transgressions.'

I gulped. 'Really? Why not?'

'Julian! What kind of question is that! It's logical, isn't it? If, let's say, your sister breaks her friend's doll, just for the fun of it, *you* can't repent that for her.'

263

'Can't I?' I picked at the grille with my finger. The painted mesh was duller at mouth-level. 'But I can . . . of course I can!'

'No, boy. Quite clearly: no. You can pray that God will forgive the one in question, lead him onto the right path and so on. But you cannot confess and repent his sins. And I cannot grant him absolution by making you pay penance. That's absurd! Don't you understand?'

I thought for a moment. Then I shook my head.

He ran both his hands through his hair. 'That's enough for now. We can talk about it at leisure another time. People are waiting . . . was there anything else?'

I didn't say anything, and he knocked against the partition.

'Hey! Stop daydreaming.'

'Yes. I mean no. The bike. I lost his bike.'

'Whose bike?'

'Well, of the man whose sins you won't forgive.'

'Julian, stop it now! I'm not *allowed* to!' A drop of spittle flew from his lip, and I saw the flashing of his glasses behind the grille. 'You can't hold everyone up like this!' He lifted two fingers, made a cross. '*Ego te absolvo*. Two Our Fathers and one Hail Mary.'

'Thanks be to God!' I whispered, and stood up. The organist had begun a quiet improvization, and I went through the church and kneeled down in the last pew. A few old women were sitting in the modern room with the slanting pillars, watching the sexton light the candles. The Eternal Light cast a red glow onto the whitewashed wall, and I said two Hail Marys and four Our Fathers. Then I went out.

All the lines on the football pitch had been renewed. A gust of wind had swept the chalk off one of the penalty spots; now it already looked a bit smudged, like a head with white hair. The man was sitting on his cart drinking from his thermos flask, and I took a demonstratively big step across the sideline. He lifted a hand in greeting.

It got warmer, and I took off my windcheater and stuffed it in the bag. As I approached Pomrehn's property, I could see from a distance that the hut wasn't there anymore. There were charred remains sticking out of the grass, and a few of them still smoked when I poked about in the ashes with a branch. I walked across the yard and called Zorro. He was nowhere in sight. But a bird squawked in the trees above me, flapped about in the leaves, and for a moment I thought I saw the cockatiel's grey feathers.

Old Pomrehn was sitting by the kitchen window rolling a cigarette. A bottle of beer on the cold coal stove. I stepped up to the balustrade.

'Hello! Who burnt down the hut?'

He shrugged his shoulders and licked the gummed paper. Though his hair looked thin, the wild bristles of his eyebrows were as thick as beetles' legs. 'Well, who d'you think . . .' He struck a match, drew the flame into the tobacco. 'Your mates of course. I suppose they felt obliged to do something really brainless. And they almost roasted the dog too.'

'Zorro?'

He blew out the smoke and nodded. 'They'd already covered him in petrol; wanted to see him run through the cornfield as a torch. Luckily there was a roof beam lying around. They won't be back in a hurry . . . where you off to with that baggage? Going on a trip?' He grinned. 'To old Manitou?'

'No idea. Maybe I'll run away. Do you know where the dog is now?'

He squinted at the sun and took another drag on his cigarette; his cheeks sank deep inwards. Then he spat out some tobacco.

'That's a stupid idea . . . running away, I mean. What are you running away from? Got yourself in trouble?'

I didn't answer. With my sandal I scratched about between the crown caps that were lying in front of the window. Some of them were shiny, others already rusty, and he took a swig of beer.

'You're Tecumseh, aren't you? And I'm old Geronimo, and I tell you: there's no running away. Wherever you go, you're in the world, my boy. And that world's always the same. So stay where you are, and if there's a storm brewing, just tell yourself: it'll pass, even the worst does.'

'You think so?'

'Sure. Who could do anything to you? The whole universe is perfect, you understand. One can't take anything away from it or add anything to it. You've long been dead and you'll always be alive.' He tapped his forehead. 'And if you've chosen freedom, nothing can happen to you. Never.'

When I turned off onto our street, I could already see it from a distance and ran faster. The heavy glass in my sports bag banged against my back with every step, but I ignored the pain. I jumped over the hedge to make the way shorter. It really was our bike standing in front of the door. The tyres were intact, the pump with the wooden handle was still fastened, and all the tools in the bag seemed to be there. The only thing missing was the bell lid with the clover imprint.

I ran up the stairs. The door was open. My father, wearing his corduroy trousers and a black T-shirt, was sitting on the sofa, and looked up only briefly. He was reading a form that was on the table in front of him, and I cleared my throat, staying in the doorway. 'I'm sorry, Dad. Didn't look for a moment, and then it was gone. It was probably the other guys in the . . . I mean, next time I'll lock it, I promise. And I'll replace the lid. With my pocket money or something. I'll go to Sterkrade, to that bike shop by the station, it's not so expensive there, and then . . .'

My father frowned; he didn't even seem to have been listening. He cast a quick glance towards the kitchen and turned over the form. Still holding the handle, I moved my head slightly forwards; the sun was shining through the cabinet, its cut glass, with the polished floorboards and a pair of brown shoes glistening behind it, and I suddenly felt as if an electric shock had gone through the roots of my hair. Leaning against the doorway, his arms and ankles crossed, was Herr Gorny. He was wearing a suit and a light blue shirt, and didn't react to my quiet 'Good morning'; he didn't even seem to notice me. His mouth was narrow, his jawbones twitched as if he were clenching his teeth, and the silence in the room grew more and more oppressive. I took a step to the side, out of their field of view.

My father was pale; he ran his thumb and forefinger over his cheeks, the vertical fold he had there, and closed his eyes for a moment. 'All right then, Konrad.' He flicked the form off the table; it sailed onto the carpet. 'We're through then, aren't we?'

He stood up, breathing heavily, and pointed to the door with his open hand. He was taller than Herr Gorny, and more handsome anyway. The hair on the back of his neck was starting to curl, the way it always did when he hadn't been to the hairdresser for a long time, the shirt was taut across his body, and strong veins wound themselves around his arms. Only the hand he reached for his cigarettes with was shaking. Very gently;

the other man wouldn't have seen it. 'And now get out of here!'

But Herr Gorny didn't move, at least not right away, just lifted his chin and narrowed his eyes. 'Now listen to me . . .' He reached into his pocket, rattled with his keys and hardly seemed to part his teeth. 'You needn't be getting cheeky now. We can sort this out another way. One phone call's enough, as you know. It's only three numbers.'

My father nodded. It looked sad, somehow as if his head were incredibly heavy. 'Okay, do what you want. I can't stop you. And now *go*. I won't say it again . . .'

Gorny pushed his left cuff back as if to look at his watch. But he wasn't wearing one, and quickly scratched the red mark on his wrist. He eyed the walls and the floor of the room as if measuring everything in his mind, pushed himself off the doorframe, which still had my pencil drawing on it, and walked casually into the hall. 'So . . .' He ran his finger along the bar separating the dado from the wallpaper and looked at it. Then he looked over to the small sharply-angled window. My mother had put a vase with straw flowers on the ledge. 'I want you out by the end of the month.'

He went down the stairs without closing our door, and I stretched out my arm to take the handle—when my father turned round and shut it with such a powerful kick that it flew open again and only just missed banging against the cabinet. I held onto it.

'What did he mean *out?*'

But he just shook his head; he seemed to be thinking. He was looking at the smoke eater, the owl with the yellow eyes that reflected the living room window. I turned round and discovered the form under the armchair. But before I could bend down and pick it up, he put a hand on my shoulder and pushed me towards the kitchen. 'I have to go in a minute. Can you make me some sandwiches?'

He went into the bathroom with his shirt already half over his head, and I took the loaf out of the box. The crank of the bread slicer squeaked, hurting my teeth, and after I had spread margarine on six slices, I couldn't find anything to put on them; the fridge was empty, and I wiped my hands on my trousers and went out onto the balcony, leaned against the railing. Tiny drops of spittle flew out of my mouth as I yawned.

A train whistled in the valley. The sound of the wheels on the rails became louder and didn't seem to

271

end; it was one of those long coal trains that made the nails you put on the track for flattening so thin that they were no use as arrowheads anymore; you could fold them like a piece of paper afterwards. But you could shape roses out of one pfennig coins. I stepped back from the railing, sat down on the chair and got a start when I suddenly found her standing behind me. Behind the curtains.

'Hey hey! Why so jumpy?' She was only mumbling. 'Guilty conscience?'

But she didn't open the drapes, and I didn't answer. I looked in front of me, to the garden, where a few titmice were chasing through the shrubs and Frau Gorny was hanging up laundry, including the sports shirt with the eagle emblem. I was tired, rubbed my eyes, and secretly hoped that she would go away or close the window. But she stayed behind me; I heard her chewing some gum and smelled her perfume, which I liked better than my mother's. But she had put on too much of it.

'If only it wasn't so hot . . .' Some paper crinkled, then she struck a match. 'But it's going to rain tomorrow.'

Then my father came into the kitchen, freshly-shaved and dressed, and I stood up and looked around from the corner of my eye. But I couldn't see her any-more. Maybe she had sat down on the bed. There was some foam stuck to his ear, and he pointed at the sand-wiches. 'What's in them?'

I closed the balcony door. 'Nothing. The fridge is empty. But if you give me some money, I'll nip down to the co-op and buy you some sausage.'

He snorted. 'You're a fine one! On the twenty-third? Put some salt on, that'll do.'

'Why are you going so early? Has something happened?'

'No, don't worry. I still have to take care of a few things. And then go to the guild.'

'You could take cold lentil soup too. Look . . .' I took the glass out of my sports bag. 'I've already filled some in here.'

'Good idea. Don't forget the spoon.'

In the cupboard I also found a chocolate from the coffee box, put it in with the sandwiches, and when I had packed his bag I put it on the sofa and sat down on the armrest. He tied his shoelaces with double bows. His hands weren't shaking anymore.

'Dad? What did Herr Gorny want? Do we have to move out?'

The bike clips clicked as he fastened them on his trouser legs. 'Well, looks like it.'

'And why? Because of me?'

He looked up. 'What? Why because of you?'

I shrugged my shoulders and took his jacket off the hook. 'But why then?'

'Oh . . . you're still too young to understand.'

'And who was he going to phone?' I insisted. 'The police?'

He didn't look at me. 'Why the police?'

'Don't know. He doesn't even have a telephone, does he?'

Now my father nodded, raised an eyebrow, and there was something fresh, something sparkling in his eyes. 'Oh, he can, does that with his accordion. If you press the right keys, it's child's play.'

I grinned, and he also gave a smile, wider than I had seen in a long time, showing his healthy teeth. He swung his jacket over his shoulders and went out. But he had barely stepped into the hall when he opened the door again, just a little. He reached through the crack, pulled the key out and put it in his pocket.

I stepped out onto the balcony again and looked after him. Marusha's window was shut. Nothing behind her window except the reflection of her mirror, and when my father turned off onto the road on the other side of the mowed fields he looked round, and I waved. He raised a hand and I rubbed my ear hard, hoping he'd do the same; I'd forgotten to tell him about the shaving foam. But he rode into the alder grove, the shadows of the leaves flickering on his back, and then he was out of sight.

The next day it rained, though not very hard. By evening it was already humid again. As always, the street filled with children as soon as Grandpa Jupp parked his car in front of the door. Sophie was the first to get out. She jumped onto the pavement, and I squatted down so that she could give me a kiss.

'Juli! You know what? I can ride without a saddle. I had a speckled pony called Murmel. It had a really, really soft snout, and those little hairs tickled whenever it ate sugar out of my hand. And I had a friend! He always gave me half of his raisin cake. Sometimes even more than that. And you know what his name is? Something really funny.' Snorting with laughter, she lowered her chin onto her neck. '*Ole*! Have you ever heard a name like that?'

She gave me a kiss, and I brushed a strand of hair from her forehead. 'Wow, you've got so many freckles. And your hair's much lighter.'

She nodded weightily. 'That's because of the sea. But I wasn't in it often. It was full of those slimy things, you know, those jollyfishes.'

'You mean jellyfish.' I straightened up and took my mother's bag. She was wearing the tight suit and a white blouse, and the smile she greeted me with looked sad; the skin around her eyes was red. The crocheted border of a handkerchief stuck out between her fingers.

'Have you grown again?'

I grinned, brushed my hair from my forehead. She wasn't wearing any lipstick, and she had more of those little veins one calls spider veins on her cheeks. All the Gornys' windows were shut, even though it was so warm, and she looked around the street; but there were no neighbours to be seen, at least no adults. Grandpa Jupp pulled her suitcase out of the car boot and closed the tailgate.

'Then off indoors with all of you! I've still got a body to take away.'

Once we were inside, my mother first of all had a look at the plants, felt the soil in the pots. Sophie ran into our room and threw the case on her bed. 'Grandma always made potato pancakes for me, Juli. If I said I wanted potato pancakes, she made some. Fried in lard. And what about you? What did you eat?'

I sat down on the edge of the bed and scratched my knees. 'Chicken. Roast chicken with chips every day. Sometimes I just nibbled the skin off. When it was really crispy.'

She looked at me in disbelief. 'Is that true? Where did you buy them? Kleine-Guck?'

I nodded, and she lifted her narrow shoulders and pushed out her lower lip briefly. 'Oh well, can't be helped—Shall I tell you something?'

'A secret?'

'Nah, anyone's allowed to know.' She picked her nose. 'I've got a beautiful soul.'

'You? Says who?'

'Ole's mother. That's right.'

'Can you see something like that? What's a soul anyway?'

'My dear boy, don't be so stupid, all right? Everyone knows that. The soul is what makes a bird sing. And shall I tell you something else?'

'No thanks.'

'I will anyway.' Now she was whispering. 'We're moving! Into a new house.'

'Seriously?'

She nodded. 'Pretty soon too. And you know why?'

'No idea. Tell me!'

'I think it's because we're underage.'

'Oh God! Where d'you get that idea from?'

'Don't know. Mum said that to Grandpa Jupp, in the car. If you're underage and you get up to no good, you get thrown out. Did you get up to no good?'

I shook my head.

'Me neither. And what's underage?'

'Well, when you're still young.'

'So I'm underage?'

'Just like me.'

'And Marusha too?'

'Her too. You're only a grown-up when you turn 16, I think. Well, maybe not quite. But then you can smoke and ride a moped and stuff like that.'

'I've smoked too!'

'You?'

She pushed down on the locks of the suitcase. 'With Ole. His father's got a white pipe, made of meerschaum, and we put in some leaves from last autumn. Didn't taste good though. Just coughed. And now . . .'

The bolts snapped open, and she opened the lid and pulled a little packet out from under the teddy. Newspaper, wrapped together with her rubber twist. 'I promised you some shells, didn't I? But there weren't any. Or just really small ones. They already broke in the swimming bag. And the sea star stank like anything! Like an askari. So . . .' She stretched out both arms. '. . . you can have this! Your welcome. My pleasure.'

Kieler Nachrichten was written on the newspaper, and of course I felt immediately what was wrapped in it. But I still pretended to be surprised. 'Wow, great! A horseshoe? Just what I've always wanted.' It was rusty

and big, probably from a farm horse, and had a row of
square holes. One of the two prongs had broken off.
'Where did you get that?'

'Well, from Ole! His father's a blacksmith. It's
brings luck, you know. I've got one too.'

I bent down, hugged her, and gave her a kiss on
the cheek. She smelled of raspberry drops and giggled.
Our mother opened the door.

'Hey, what's all this?'

I showed her the horseshoe. 'Just saying thank you.'

Then I stood up, and she stared at me as if she suddenly suspected something. Her eyes were moist again.
'Come quickly to say goodbye to Grandpa Jupp, you
two.'

We went into the living room. With his arms
crossed, he was standing with his back to the wall and
looking around the room. The brim of his sailor's cap
shone greasily.

'Well, I think a 7.5 tonne truck should do it. For
those few bits and pieces . . . it's nothing. I'll come on
Saturday, fairly early, and on Sunday you can already
have breakfast in the new place. Like I said, it's really
pretty. Central heating. You'll like it.'

My mother nodded. I thought she was going to say something, but she just took a shaky breath. She was holding the handkerchief under her nose, and Grandpa Jupp buttoned up his overall. 'Come on girl, get a hold of yourself! It can happen. More often in the best families than the worst. Men are stags, they need a herd. You think I was any different? Martha had a lot to put up with, I can tell you. Though strictly speaking I saved her a lot of trouble that way. But when it comes down to it—should you go worrying about that? Is it worth it? In the end we'll all be sharing the same bed anyway, deep down under the ground.'

My mother sniffled and gulped, and Sophie reached for her hand. When she looked up at her I saw two vertical folds between her eyebrows, very delicate, like the veins in leaves; I had never seen them before. 'What is it, Mum?'

She shook her head, pushed the handkerchief under her cuff. 'Nothing, sweetie, nothing. I'm just wondering if they'll fit, the curtains. It was all tailor-made, after all.'

'Oh come on. If it doesn't fit, we'll make it fit!' Grandpa Jupp ruffled my hair. 'Isn't that right, my little corpse-washer?'

His hand was heavy on my head, and I turned it away and said: 'Nah.'

His laugh sounded a bit dirty. 'I can understand that. Don't pay anything, do I? And these dead bodies are boring as hell. Just lie there, never opening their mouths. Instead of talking about something . . . they just make those sour faces, let us fold their hands and brush their eyebrows, and the likes of us don't even get a thank you. All right then, folks, see you on Saturday. Take care!'

He went downstairs slowly, step by step, and the stairs creaked. My sister and I watched him squeeze behind the wheel of his Mercury and take a cigar from the glove compartment. The sun was already setting, but he didn't turn on the lights yet; he turned slowly at the end of the street, and the windows all around, the lights from the kitchen and the living room, made distorted reflections in the finish. One could hardly hear the motor.

There was potato salad and sliced goose breast for supper. My mother had brought lard, half a ham and some home-smoked sausages and trouts too, but didn't eat anything herself. She sat down with us and smoked. There was a light grey stain on the collar of her blouse, maybe from a tear, with a bit of mascara, and suddenly she looked at me.

'Did anything come in the mail? From Spar?'

I didn't answer, just stared at my plate, and she brushed the ash off her cigarette and leaned forwards. 'What? What is it? Have you got something stuck in your throat? Sophie, quick! Give your brother a slap on the back!'

But I put her off and drank some milk. 'It's all right, thanks.'

'You two be careful, you hear. There could be bone splinters in the goose breast. Grandma's no butcher, you know. She chops those animals like wood. Make sure you watch out.'

Buttermilk, ice cold. My swallow made a hard sound. 'Why Spar?' I spoke into my glass, and my mother waved her hand about above the table. But the smoke hardly moved.

'What, didn't I tell you? I applied there. They're looking for some temporary help, part-time. And God knows we could use the money. Now more than ever.'

After supper she cleared the table, but didn't wash the dishes straight away. She joined us on the couch, and we played a few rounds of animal quartet. But her mind was somewhere else. She put the even-toed ungulates together with the predatory cats, and twice she had the white rabbit without telling us. Then we watched *Hier und Heute*. But she sent us to bed even before the news, and when we had brushed our teeth she turned off the light.

I wasn't tired yet, and for a while I waited in vain for Sophie to go to sleep. Normally I could tell by her breathing. Then I could switch on my torch and read. But then she sat up.

'Juli?' she whispered.

'Mmh?' There was only a slim strip of light in the room, but I saw her big eyes, gleaming like mother-of-pearl.

'You know what? I don't want to move house.'

'Why not? The new place is nice.'

'Have you had a look yet?'

'No. Dad says we've both got rooms of our own.'

'Does it have a garden?'

'I doubt it. But you haven't got one here either.'

'Yes I have!'

'No, it's not ours. And I'd rather have no garden at all than one that doesn't belong to me.'

'Well, I do want one. So where are we supposed to play?'

'The heath is right behind the estate. And the idiot hill. You can go there with roller skates. And it's not that far to school either.'

'Oh yeah? Okay. But listen, I'm only moving into the new flat if it's got a balcony. And one of those nice toilet roll holders. At Grandma's the roll just lay on the floor, and you couldn't flush. Everything just plopped down and stank.'

'Why? What's so special about our toilet roll holder?'

She lay down again. 'Come on, you know that! The tile that sort of goes round and in. I always like putting a new roll in there. It fits just right. You think there'll be something like that in the flat too?'

'I'm sure there will,' I said. 'The houses are all the same.' And finally she sighed; it sounded relieved. Then she laid an arm across her eyes and was already asleep.

I read for a while, then got up as quietly as I could to drink a glass of milk. I tiptoed through the hall. The living room was only dimly lit by the street lamp on the other side of the street. My mother's clothes, her skirt and blouse, were hanging over an armchair, her stockings dangling from the backrest of the other one. She herself was lying on the couch under a woollen blanket. Her bare shoulders looked white in the twilight, and she was still wearing her pearl necklace. There was no cigarette between her fingers or glowing in the ashtray; but she wasn't asleep. She turned her head.

'What's the matter?' I whispered. 'Are you sleeping here?'

I couldn't make out her eyes, and she gulped and turned away again. 'Go to bed,' she mumbled, and I took another step. The floorboard creaked. But suddenly I didn't dare go to the kitchen anymore. I opened the bathroom door and drank some water from the tap. Then I went to bed.

The man opened the barrier. This part of the drift hadn't been cleared out any more. They'd sprinkled salt here to bind the explosive coal dust, the way they often did when there was a high humidity level—salt that crystallized after a while and kept sealing new dust particles inside itself. The carapaces cracked underfoot, the taste on his lips grew stronger, and soon the whole drift, the level, the stopes and the ridge, as well as some of the tools looked frozen, as if under hoarfrost. A spring hook, impossible to budge. A shrivelled-up glove. Wherever he looked, the rock sparkled in the light of his headlamp, and sometimes the shine was so bright that he squeezed his eyes together. As if light were growing here, young light in tiny crystals.

The level sloped down, and the man held onto the props; he could hardly even make out the wood they were made of. They stood on either side of the beam of light from his headlamp like a row of alabaster pillars, and he licked his lips again. It was quiet here, and when he stood still and the grinding of his shoes on the ground stopped, he could only hear the humming from the ventilation shaft far behind him. His breath burned in his nose. Between two props there was a cage, slightly squashed. That was no rat trap; he could make out the perch and the bowl, and when he bent down and closed the door, salt burst out of the wire and the hinges. But other than that, he couldn't move it.

His father had told him about them, and even he only knew through hearsay. Because they didn't trust the safety lamps and the new measuring instruments, old miners kept bringing songbirds underground with them, preferably canaries. The birds were so sensitive that even the slightest fluctuations in the oxygen level, for example if gas was escaping, made them stop singing and fall down unconscious in their cages. And then it was time to run, run, and open all the air shafts!

The coal at the end of the face was white with salt, and he turned on his spare lamp and put it on the ground. The condition of the rock hadn't changed much; the fissure had hardly grown. But nothing was dripping out of it anymore; the level and the side walls were almost dry. He only saw a little dead water gleaming in some of the recesses, and he stopped under the last cap and listened. Here, behind the bend in the old coal face, he couldn't hear the air anymore either, and he lifted his head so that the light from his headlamp would shine further into the fissure.

The armchairs had been put on the couch, the curtains taken down, and the carpet rolled up. Sophie, on her knees, was rummaging about in a box full of books, magazines and albums, and my mother took the shopping bag off me and weighed it in her hand. I nodded. 'Frau Kalde says hello. She didn't give me a beer, and would like you to . . .'

'Yes, yes, not now. Help me with the table.'

We went out onto the balcony. The red sunset behind the mine was reflected in Marusha's half-opened window. She was standing in front of a board in her dressing gown ironing. My mother ignored her and indicated with a severe glance that I shouldn't look into the room. The Graham Bonney cut-out was still missing one foot. We lifted the table through the doorway, brought it into the living room, and Sophie leapt up.

'Look what I found, Mum! Julian in the snow, in shorts! When did you take that?'

It was a postcard-sized photo, though the actual picture was an oval. My mother put plates on the table and frowned, wrinkling her painted eyebrows.

'Oh, nonsense! Can't you see that it's old?' She took it away from her and looked at the back. '1936. Your father was 12.'

'But he looks like Juli, doesn't he? The hair, the eyes . . . just like him! But why's he got shorts on? It's winter.'

'That's how it was in the old days. But he's wearing long socks, isn't he. Tidy that stuff up, please.' She put the cutlery around the table and gave me a quick look out of the corner of her eye. There was a strand dangling in front of her forehead, and suddenly she spoke in a muted voice, as if she didn't want my sister to hear.

'So tell me, what else happened while I was away? Who was in here?'

I took a step back and shrugged. Then I bent down and helped Sophie clear up the books. 'Why? Who would have been here? Nobody.'

'Oh really?' She pointed to the corner next to the broom cupboard. 'And what's that?'

I looked round. The weather house was standing on a chair. Underneath were a shovel and brush. 'What do you mean?'

She clenched her teeth, just on one side, and grew pale. Her whole body tensed up, and the heels of her sandals, wedges of pressed cork, rattled on the floorboards as she came around the table and pulled me away from the box. 'I want to know what exactly I've *swept up* here!'

I raised an elbow to cover my face. 'No idea. What is it? Hair?'

'Of course it is! You don't have to tell me that, idiot. But whose hair? Is it animal hair? Don't tell me you've had a mutt in here!'

I tried to free myself from her grip. But her nails only dug further into my arm. 'No! Or wait—yes, just once. Zorro. He's a hunting dog from the animal club. He was really well-behaved. I just gave him a quick bath . . .'

'You did what?' She pulled at me, squeezing her eyes together. 'You can't be serious! In our bathtub? Where we wash ourselves every day and I soak my stockings and knickers—and you put a dirty, flea-ridden . . .'

'I washed it out! With hot water and cleaner. I even did it twice.'

Her eyes were as rigid as glass, her lips no more than a line. She pushed me into the corner and pulled open the drawer with the wooden spoons. But it had already been cleared out, and when, after stopping short for a moment, she realized she had forgotten that, it only made her angrier. It only took a single movement to close it again with her hip and bend down for the hand brush. Unlike its felt bristles, the dark back of the brush was as shiny as new, except for a few semicircular dents. I had used it a while ago to hammer the drawing pins for my poster into the wall, and as she took a swing I already lost a drop of urine.

I wanted to squat down, but she held me tight. Her face was right in front of mine, and as she spoke I could only see her lower teeth. And the throbbing of her jugular vein.

'Can't I rely on you even once? The minute I'm gone you're up to no good. The house turns into a pigsty, the plants dry up, there's dirt on the stairs, and then you bring that filthy animal in here and poison everything with hair . . .' Her blouse smelled of lavender, and once again she changed her position, standing with her legs as far apart as her tight skirt allowed. 'Why d'you think I'm sick all the time? Well? Why am I going out of my bloody mind with stress? Sometimes I could really . . .'

I turned my face away, lifted my knee and covered my bottom with my free hand. But there wasn't much space in the corner; first she hit the stove, then the poker hanging on the rail. It rattled against the enamel.

'Leave him alone, Mum! Please, leave him!'

There was a pleading in my sister's voice. She waved the photo about as if trying to distract us, and for a moment I saw my own face fluttering through the light and the shadows. The silhouette in the snow. Pigeons were flying through the sunset, and the two wheels in the winding tower, which had been moving in contrary motion only a moment before, stood still.

'Come on Mum, we're moving house!'

My mother breathed so deeply that her nostrils flared. The corners of her eyes filled with water, and she opened her mouth, relaxing her grip. I moved back between the cupboard and the sink, and with trembling hands she lowered the brush and put it on the stove.

'What was that?' Sophie turned round, but my mother took no notice of her. She took a cigarette out of the packet, went onto the balcony and lit up. Threw the match over the railing. 'There it is again!' My sister, wide-eyed, pointed to the corner. The glasses rattled against each other, just for a moment, and we listened out for a truck on the street. But there was no sound.

I felt sick. I sat down on the book box, and she put an arm around my shoulders and nudged my ear with her nose. Her whispers felt as if they had wings.

'You see, the horseshoe brought you luck, didn't it?' Her breath smelled sweet, and I nodded, wiped the sweat from my brow and dried my fingers on my shirt. No wet patch on my trousers.

Then she held the photo up next to my face, laid her head first on her left, then her right shoulder, and while she compared the two she nibbled at her lower lip. The blue of her eyes seemed to grow even brighter, and suddenly she lifted a finger and gave a broad grin. I'd heard keys too, the front door opening, the heavy steps coming up the stairs, and she whirled around. 'Mum, get supper ready! Dad's coming!'

A sparkling and flashing, crystalline. The man locked a drill rod in the pneumatic hammer and dragged the air tube along the level. The impact piston clicked in the cylinder, and he opened the box with the detonating equipment and counted the aluminium capsules. They were encased in polystyrene, and would be enough for two holes several metres deep. Enough for a butterfly blast, and he put the hammer on a drill wagon and pushed it against the end wall of the drift. That way he could risk a breakthrough without having to step under the hanging wall.

It was hot there; he took off his jacket and continued work in his vest. When he opened the pneumatic valve, the recoil was weaker than he had expected. He could keep the hammer in position by the hose, and the tip wound its way into the stone with a screeching, a sound that turned into a rumbling as the drill went deeper, while bore dust accumulated on the level—first grey, then deep black, then a reddish grey. A little over an hour later he had drilled the first hole, and was satisfied. There wasn't even any salt trickling from the ridge, and he pushed the wagon one metre further and got started on the second hole.

Once the tip was in far enough to stay in position by itself, he went back behind the hydraulic station and set the detonator, checked the tension and laid the cable. The drill was already up to the fitting spring in the rock, probably forge coal; the dust in front of the wheels shone black, and he closed the valve and pulled the wagon out of the drift. Then he took the charges from the box—one at a time, with both hands—and pushed five in each hole; then the short detonating caps, filled with mercury fulminate and connected by thin cables; and then another two charges. Finally he sealed everything up with a clay stopper about a foot long that was in one of the buckets next to the box, and knocked it in with the handle of his mallet.

He looked at his watch, blowing the dust from the cracked glass. He still had time. The blast would only be authorized in half an hour, as the gauge doors were still open. He took off his gloves and sat down on the empty ammunition box, leaned back and turned off his headlamp to save battery power.

The sudden blackness was like a cool hand on his eyelids. His sweat tasted saltier than usual. He heard himself breathing in the silence, crossed his arms and thought wearily about the expression 'butterfly blast', and about the fact that he had never done one before. Things like that were only found in manuals. His blast-holes had all sorts of shapes, but they never looked like butterflies, and he put his helmet down beside him and nodded off.

He slept lightly and only for a few minutes, but when he woke up—something had moved near him—he tried in vain, for the duration of a few pounding heart-beats, to open his eyes. Until he realized that they were already open, and turned on his headlamp.

Heat. The gauge doors shut one by one. And then, in the sudden silence, it was there again after all, and he held his breath, stood up and approached the hanging wall. He held on to a prop, and his helmet scraped against the last crossbeam, which had already sunk down slightly, a cracked spruce under the crevasses in the ledge; it hadn't grown together with the rock. Salt trickled down the back of his neck. But he wanted to get closer to the sound, that quiet whirring, or whatever it was. He moved his head forward, listening . . .

You don't hear it, the stone that hits you. Even with your steel caps and heavy belt equipment, you take a fast, almost ecstatic step, as if you thought you could get back behind that second again. But in fact you're not even on your feet anymore. Your helmet rolls forward, the headlamp glass shatters, and the light gleams for an instant in the salt. And then it's dark.

Last of all I took the bird poster off the wall. It had hung in the sun, and the colours had already faded slightly. But I rolled it up, put it in the box in the hall, and then swept my room. In the corner lay a little sheet of tracing paper, that Sophie used to copy the figures from her

297

Fix und Foxi comics, and a few broken shells. There were two pfennigs and a hairpin between the joints of the reddish brown floor tiles, but they were stuck. Suddenly the room felt very big. There was no wallpaper, and the paint seemed lighter where the poster had hung. I swept everything across the threshold and looked round again. There was nothing left in the room; even the light bulb had been taken out of its socket. Then I whistled a bit to hear the reverberations, which I enjoyed. I whistled louder, even managed a sort of trill, in several different registers, and slowly the clouds drifted away from the window. A thin ray of light shot in, dust particles danced in the sunbeams, and suddenly the birds—all the titmice, bullfinches and orioles—were there again. Gossamer and grey, like a watermark on the wall.